THE SCENT OF SALT & SAND

AN ESCAPED NOVELLA

KRISTIN CAST
& P.C. CAST

D0059661

DIVERSIONBOOKS

Also in the Escaped Series
Amber Smoke
Scarlet Rain

Diversion Books
A Division of Diversion Publishing Corp.
443 Park Avenue South, Suite 1008
New York, New York 10016
www.DiversionBooks.com

For more information, email info@diversionbooks.com

First Diversion Books edition October 2016.
Print ISBN: 978-1-68230-343-6
eBook ISBN: 978-1-68230-342-9

This book is dedicated to our House of Night fans!
We heard you when you asked for more.
Happy reading to the most loyal fans in the world!

PROLOGUE

Once, when the world was young and wild, and immortals walked beside mortals, Achelous, the most ancient and feared of the river gods, fell in love with Calliope, the exquisite Muse of epic poetry. Their affair was brief, but passionate. The gods loved with such blazing desire that, as with any all-consuming fire, their love extinguished on a pyre of self-absorption.

This fleeting union bore daughters named Sirens, demigods who reflected their parents' divine nature. Like their mother, they were preternaturally beautiful, gifted with voices that even the Muses envied, for they also had the ability to mold the wills of men.

From their river god father, they were gifted with the ability to shift their forms, so that they could always find solace in any of the waters of the earth. But their father's powerful nature was not as easily contained as was their birthright from their more refined mother. Achelous was one of the oldest of the gods—brother to the mighty Titans—so hidden beneath the surface loveliness of Calliope's daughters lurked a predatory nature, so base a beast that mankind had no choice but to fall prey to them.

Calliope built her beloved daughters a magnificent palace on an island called Anthemoessa. Achelous was devoted to them as well, and convinced Poseidon to allow the Sirens to hunt in the mighty ocean god's waters.

At first all was well—the Sirens prospered. Calliope was well pleased by the stories told of their beauty and their magical voices. Achelous was well pleased by the stories told of their prowess as huntresses, for in his watery world the weak must fall to the strong.

Time passed and the world changed. Still the Sirens prospered. They learned to hide their true nature under the ruse of beauty, but that ruse only worked as long as their human prey did not glimpse what waited beneath their gentle façade. As with all gifts given by the gods, they came with a price. In order to mate and procreate, the Sirens had to revert to their True Form, and that visage was so terrifying, so fantastically, unbelievably horrible, that humans responded on a visceral level—their minds were unable to comprehend the truth of the Sirens, and they went utterly mad. It became a mercy for the Sirens to kill each time they loved.

Some Sirens rebelled. They weren't murderers. They only desired peace and the love of a mate, but allowing a human to see a True Form and live proved impossible. If they weren't driven mad, the men were still utterly changed, and that change put the Sirens in danger of being hunted and exterminated, for though they were the daughters of immortals and as such had the ability to live for centuries, they could be killed if they were beheaded or burned on land.

Perhaps it was because they could not love without death, or perhaps it was because their father's nature proved stronger than their mother's, but over the eons the Sirens became comfortable with their design—they perfected their killing techniques, and nurtured the terrible myth that was their story.

Eventually, power did as it is wont to do—it corrupted. The Sirens reveled in their power over men, drawing more and more humans to their remote isle, toying with them, loving them, and ending them.

The wives of slain sailors began to pray. They beseeched Hera, the mother of Olympus. Over and over the mortal women begged the goddess to help them—to contain the Sirens—to end their reign of terror.

Hera heard her worshipers and called on the Furies to aid her. The Furies agreed with the mother of Olympus— the Sirens must be contained for the good of the Mortal Realm, but they also understood that, unlike the monsters and murderers that filled the immortal hell of Tartarus, the Sirens were not responsible for the nature gifted to them by their father. So the Furies decided that they would create a special cove for them at the edge of Tartarus, where they would be allowed to live out eternity frolicking within the confines of the Underworld. Hera agreed, with one slight addition to the Furies' plan. She, who understood the cleverness of the Sirens' predatory nature, cursed them. As long as they remained in Tartarus, they would stay eternally young and beautiful, but should they ever enter the Mortal Realm again, they would immediately begin to age,

KRISTIN CAST & P.C. CAST

sicken, and eventually die a mortal death. Then, with one swift stroke from the mother of Olympus, the Sirens were banished from the Mortal Realm for eternity.

No matter how lovely a prison is, it is still a prison. The Sirens waited in their forced exile, planning and plotting with the brilliance of a Muse and the patience of an immortal, until one day Tartarus fell ill, and their prison weakened, allowing a glimmer of the Mortal Realm to shine through the veil that separated them from their truest desire—freedom.

Whispers from a world both foreign and seductive slipped through the veil, illuminating their gilded cage with a marvelous knowledge of a new magic called *technology.*

The Sirens continued to watch and wait as they learned everything they could about the modern mortal world—and as they waited, the tear in the veil unraveled enough to allow a few of them at a time to secretly slip from their prison to the Mortal Realm.

The journey was fraught with danger, which did not end once they arrived. The curse was upon them then, and they aged swiftly, which forced them to return to their prison in the Underworld.

But the Sirens were wise. They had a plan. *They* had been cursed by Hera—their children had not been. It became their mission—their obsession—to mate with mortal men over and over through generations until the blood that tied them to their mothers' curse was diluted enough to allow a new breed of Siren to exist, free and powerful once more, in the modern world.

The Sirens understood that it might take decades, centuries even, to produce children who could survive in the modern world, but immortality breeds patience, and the Sirens had become very, *very* patient.

This time they would be more careful.

This time they would be successful.

This time, no one would stop them.

CHAPTER ONE

"What the hell is going on over there?" Dean nodded toward the line stretching down three blocks.

"Mystique," Kait grumbled.

"Mystique? I thought that club was only open on weekends. It's Tuesday."

"They're having one of their costume parties. They're all the rage."

Clueless, Dean shrugged.

"Man, you have got to get a life outside this job." Kait slowed the police car to a crawl. "You seeing what I'm seeing?"

"Open containers," Dean sighed as a young woman tripped and toppled to the sidewalk, sending a half-empty liquor bottle shattering on the concrete. "At the very least."

"They'd have a much better night if they just waited a few more minutes until they were inside," Kait huffed as she flashed the lights and pulled the cruiser over.

As the two officers climbed out of the car, a young man

stepped out of line and locked eyes with Dean. Anxiety pinched his features—a look Dean knew all too well after years of patrolling the streets of San Francisco. "Lesnek," he called to his partner. "We might have a problem over here."

The glaring guy fidgeted with his jacket, the white fabric switching to red then blue in the lights.

"Don't do it," Dean muttered, pushing the car door closed.

The man bolted, throwing a small baggie into the steady flow of traffic.

"Lesnek!" Dean shouted. "He threw something into the street!"

"Got it! I'll follow you in the car!"

Blood pulsed behind his ears, interrupted only by Kait, calling in the pursuit to dispatch.

Dean launched himself down the street after the man in the white jacket. "Stop! SFPD!" he shouted as White Jacket turned a blind corner. Dean followed, weapon drawn. "Stop!" He repeated the order as the man disappeared over a rusted metal fence.

Following the perpetrator's lead, Dean climbed onto a dumpster and thrust himself over the chain link. Dean landed on the pavement and forced his legs to resume running, ignoring the pain barking in his ankles. White Jacket had a bigger lead now, and he took advantage of it, darting into another alleyway. Dean pumped his arms faster, willing his legs to join the quickened pace. He turned the corner. Nothing. "Shit!" he spat, peering down the narrow corridors on his right and left. "I lost him," he exhaled into the radio. "Behind the abandoned Walgreens warehouse."

He cursed again, kicking an empty can with the toe of his boot.

"Help me." A weak groan twisted in the air around Dean.

He raised his weapon, letting it lead him down one of the narrow walkways White Jacket had used to escape.

"Quiet! Be still!" Sharp hisses emanated from a dark corner of the alley.

Dean clicked his flashlight on.

Air fled his lungs as he stared, unblinking, at the creature looming on all fours over a trembling victim. "Step back!" He tried to shout, but wasn't sure if the words even left his lips.

The creature's violet scales lifted like the scruff of a dog as it screeched, and drove its long teeth into the thin flesh of the man's neck. Blood sprayed through air, splattering against the concrete.

Dean fired once, twice. The boom of the gun pierced his ears and rattled his bones.

The fanged monster shrieked and hurled itself at him, knocking him on his back before scurrying up the nearest building like a spider. Dean rolled to his stomach, searching the black pavement for his gun. Sirens wailed in the distance as he found the cool metal. He lifted the pistol, but it was too late. The creature was gone, leaving Dean in a pool of thick blood.

CHAPTER TWO

Melody took a deep breath and dove into the cobalt waters. The velvety liquid swallowed her, and she remained still, sinking, until the jutting peaks of the shoreline were a wavering mirage on the surface. Gentle vibrations hummed along her skin as its True Form took hold, sending waves of relaxation coursing through her limbs. She curled into a ball, somersaulting weightlessly. Through the light-streaked water, deep emerald scales seemed to twist and dance on her legs. She wiggled her toes, which had sprouted an almost translucent webbing since submersion.

A body dropped into the water. Waves pushed against Melody, forcing her farther from shore. She kicked to combat the pulse of the water and steer herself away from her sisters, who bobbed around her like ducks.

She forced a puff of air out of her nose. Bubbles fled to the surface, tickling her forehead along the way. With most everyone back from the Mortal Realm, the pool felt small. It was better when a dozen of them were gone. Then she could snake through the saltwater without worrying about collisions. But the pool would be crowded for one more day, until another group was selected to make the hellacious journey above. Fear flapped within her chest. She was now old enough to be chosen.

Her legs collided with something hard.

Melody! Water muted the word, but annoyance stayed hooked to it.

She popped her head out of the water.

"Gah, Melody, watch where you're going. You almost kicked me in the face."

Melody waded to shallower water and pressed her feet into the sandy waterbed. "Sorry, Arietta. I didn't see you." She smiled.

"Ugh." Arietta's cheeks were pink with youth, but her dark eyes were dulled from decades of struggle. "You always have that stupid grin on your face."

Staring at her elders made Melody's stomach sink with foreboding. She averted her gaze. "I'm just happy to be at home."

Arietta scoffed. "*Home?* You're too young to remember the meaning of the word."

"It's not so bad here. We have light, and water, and—"

"Stop right there. You must be joking." Arietta pointed to the sky. Mossy brown scales glinted on her arm, the same color as her eyes. "*That* is *not* the sun. And *this* is *not* the ocean." She slapped the surface of the water. "I hope I'm chosen again. Better yet, I hope *you're* chosen." Arietta swam away, her deliberate kicks spraying water onto Melody.

Melody stood in the shadow of Arietta's words.

She tried to find her smile, but her lips only twitched

slightly. Arietta had lived centuries longer than Melody. She'd had free reign in the Mortal Realm along with others, including Melody's mother. With the thought, Melody's shoulders slumped, and her gaze fell to the water.

She stared at her reflection, calling upon memories of the woman she missed every day. They had the same snowy skin, deep green eyes, and bright copper hair. Often she was told that she looked like Melisma's clone.

"You're my mini me," her mother used to say, and rest her forehead against Melody's. She closed her eyes, inhaling the ghost of her mother's scent, salt and sand. Her mother's smell was vibrant and alive, not like the dull scents that blew through this section of Tartarus. It used to tickle her nose and bring goose bumps to her skin.

Melody opened her eyes. Wrinkles formed on the bridge of her thin nose as joy again rested within her.

"I just got the list of names from Rhapsody herself. You ready to tell the lucky girls?"

Allegra's chipper words emanated from the alcove behind Melody, bouncing off of the cave walls, which made it almost impossible to have a private conversation anywhere. Like the others, Melody had learned to ignore the chatter. But Rhapsody was a name she couldn't disregard.

Melody gathered her thick strawberry hair and peeked over her shoulder. Harmony's gray eyes caught hers. She stifled a nervous cough.

Harmony released a tired sigh. "It's already time to make the journey again?"

No. Noiselessly, Melody exited the pool and tiptoed onto shore.

"Can't keep Siren Tours closed down for too long. It's bad for business," Allegra noted.

"You're right," Harmony said, refreshed. "Let me see the names."

Melody hurried along the crescent-shaped shoreline until she was well out of the women's path. She darted to a large boulder, and squatted down beside it. If they didn't see her, maybe she'd be passed over.

"*Melody?*" The word was a whisper. "No, Allegra, not yet. Do you even think she's ready?"

Melody wrapped her arms around her shins and squeezed tight. Her feet sank deeper into the sand, along with her hope of going another season without having to travel to the Mortal Realm.

"It really doesn't matter what I think, or you for that matter. We all had to go above when we reached twenty-five." Allegra released a sharp breath. "It's her turn."

Melody pinched her eyes shut.

"But she seems so young." Harmony's soft tone steadily echoed off the craggy walls.

"She's naïve. All of our younger sisters are. They can't remember a time before Tartarus. What we lost…" Allegra cleared her throat. "But you'll be there to teach her what's to be done."

"Yeah." Harmony paused. "Her mother and I were close. Let me tell her."

Melody's chest tightened as her heart beat ferociously. Why hadn't she run, chosen a proper place to hide? But what did it matter? Their cove was so small. She wouldn't have remained hidden for long.

Harmony's shadow fell over her. "Melody?" Her fingertips rested on Melody's quivering shoulder. "Mel?"

She shrugged. "You know I don't like to be called Mel."

Harmony squatted in front of her, displacing the sand, which buried Melody's feet in its cool depths.

"It's your time."

Slowly, Melody opened her eyelids and met Harmony's gaze. "Can't it wait? You yourself said I'm too young."

"I said you *seem* young. This place has that effect. Your experiences have been so limited. But it's time to grow up." Like always, Harmony's smile was soft and warm. It was nearly impossible to be mad or afraid when she turned it on. Melody had decided long ago that that smile was the main reason her mother had chosen Harmony to look after her.

"But what if what happened to Mom happens to me?"

"Traveling to the Mortal Realm is dangerous, but what happened to your mom doesn't happen often. Plus, I'll be there to protect you."

"Promise?"

"Definitely." She stood and offered Melody her hand. "Now, let's go tell the others the good news. It'll make you feel better."

She followed Harmony and Allegra as they found each girl and told her she had been chosen to go above. They squealed and laughed and hugged. But Melody felt hollow.

• • •

"Is everyone ready?" Harmony threw up her arms and cheered.

Melody bounced between the girls sandwiched next to

her as they gaily whooped and hopped up and down. She forced aside the dread swelling within her and clapped softly.

"Okay, okay." Harmony held a finger in front of her lips. "Just a bit more housekeeping, and then we'll get in the water." She stepped back, clearing room on the invisible stage for the woman who'd been lurking in the background.

Rhapsody stepped forward. Her predatory gaze swept over the row of young Sirens. "I have chosen well." Her smile was stiff, forced. "It seems all my girls are excited to seize their birthright. Well, *most* of you." Her eyes flicked to Melody. "To any who might be *afraid*"—Rhapsody snarled at the word—"I assure you that will slip away the moment a human is under your control. You fear the unknown, not the acts you are to perform. Those are innate, instinct."

Melody stepped further back in line, trying to escape Rhapsody's fiery glances.

"Find a suitable genetic specimen, obtain his seed, exterminate him, and repeat until it's time for you to return to Tartarus. Listen to your Caretaker"—she motioned to Harmony, who stepped up to join her—"and make us proud."

Harmony led a short applause. "Now it's time to make the journey. I'll channel the power of the Omphalos, which will allow us passage to the seas of the human world."

Linked to the sacred city of Delphi and the all-consuming power of the Titans, the Omphalos's magic remained unmatched even after the Titans were jailed and the new god, Apollo, smote the great stone. This god of the oracles scattered the stone's remnants around the Mortal Realm in an attempt to hide them from the primeval deities who could use those pieces to gain power if they were ever to escape the great prison within Tartarus.

Each of Melody's tutors had a different story of how Rhapsody found the sacred stone, but the truth was a secret only Rhapsody knew.

"You all know the potential danger, so keep your eyes open and stay together." Harmony bounced as she spoke. "What are you waiting for? Get in the water, and dive to the deepest section of the pool. As soon as you're all in, I'll join you and we'll be on our way."

Everyone leaped into the water. Everyone except Melody. She stood frozen on the shore.

"Your mom talked about this day from the moment you were born." Harmony took her hand, guiding her slowly into the waves. "She would be so happy to see you here, about to make your first journey."

Together they slipped under the surface and cut through the water to meet the others. The school of Sirens continued to swim deeper and deeper until Tartarus's light no longer pierced the vast blue. Bright white sliced through the bleak depths, and Harmony ushered them into the warm rays. Melody slowed and let her sisters swim through the tear between realms, terrified she wouldn't make it through to the other side. When she could no longer see the kicking legs of the final Siren, she set her jaw and charged through the break. The waves were more forceful on the other side. They pulled and pushed her body as she struggled to fit with the new, wilder rhythm. She relaxed a bit, seeing her sisters struggle to merge with the ocean's tireless ebb and flow. Fighting against it wouldn't work. Instead, she melted into the waves, and stretched out her fingers and toes, pulling the thin webbing taut. At ease in the savage flow, she closed her hands and took in the foreign ocean.

A ghostly figure bounced off a couple of the girls, unnoticed by them. Melody watched the strange specter navigate the waters with precision.

"Har—" Melody started to call out, to warn Harmony and the others, but the shadow bolted toward her. She tried to swim away, but hadn't found her stride in the choppy waters.

Fear clawed at Melody's chest as she bucked and kicked against the dense, dark mass. She opened her mouth to scream, but warm water filled the void and surged down her throat.

Please! A woman's voice, small and frightened, echoed through the water around her. *I need your help.*

Warmth continued down her throat, seeping into her core, electrifying her limbs until they shot out from her trunk, strong and solid like the points of a star.

This was it. The end. Her mom must have also heard that same small voice right before she met her death.

Please. You have to help me.

The words echoed between her ears. *Inside* her.

Blurry hands reached out to her, and her arms listlessly floated to meet them. They wrapped around her wrists and yanked her forward. She breached the surface. Cool air caressed her skin. And then she saw the sun. She squinted. Arietta was right. The light in Tartarus in no way compared to the glorious yellow orb floating in its own sea of cloudless blue.

"You nearly scared the pee out of me!" Dot said, her wide eyes searching Melody's. "Sorry I yanked you out of the water like that. I thought you were dead."

Melody's arms and legs ceased trembling, and she let go of Dot's forearms to tread next to her. "I thought I was too."

Dot nodded. "That was a rough swim, but at least we're here now." She sniffed the air. "You smell that?"

Melody inhaled and was instantly revitalized. The tangy scent of salt and sand swirled around her, bringing her closer to the memory of her mother. "It's amazing."

"Right?!"

Melody's grin faded. "Dot, were you just asking me for my help underwater?"

Dot shook her head. "You were struggling. You probably called out and were so scared you thought the voice was someone else's." She motioned toward shore, where the others swam a few hundred yards away. "We better catch up. Don't want to miss anything."

Melody looked around, her eyes wider and more frightened than Dot's had been. Buildings shot up from the ground, piercing the sky and reflecting stars of light like shimmering metal crystals. Cars and humans crept along congested cement trails while barnacle-bottomed boats bobbed by the docks. The city was congested and busier than any of her teachers could've prepared her for. "I need a minute."

"Okay." Dot started to swim away, but turned back. A mixture of pity and concern creased her brow. "Melisma would be proud of you." She disappeared under the water.

Melody stuck her face in the cool blue and swam toward the pier. Annoyed, she kicked forcefully and sent a cloud of agitated white water billowing around her. Next time she had to make the journey, she wouldn't let the fear of what had happened to her mom get to her.

CHAPTER THREE

"What's wrong with him?" The old bartender peered from under bushy white brows at Dean.

"Officer Kent here thinks he saw some kind of alien booger monster." Kait jabbed at his ribs with her elbow.

"I know it wasn't an alien. Or a damn booger monster." He rubbed at his side. "It was probably some woman in a costume on her way to Mystique," he said, ignoring the pinching in his gut that told him what had seen was real.

"Well, whoever it was, it's Homicide's problem and not ours. Good thing, too, because it's definitely off the crazy scale." Kait sipped her drink. "This is the best coffee in the entire fucking world. Seriously. The. Best." Kait wrapped her hands around the tall-stemmed glass etched with *Buena Vista Café San Francisco* and sipped slowly, savoring the last steaming, sticky drop.

"Best coffee or Irish whiskey?" Dean's eyes smiled at his partner over the rim of his own glass while he downed the strong, hot concoction, glad to change the subject away from the nightmare murder he'd witnessed—also glad his hands had stopped shaking.

"Does it really matter as long as my boyfriend C over there behind the bar keeps them coming?" Kait raised her voice so that the old barkeep shot her a practiced look, the perfect mixture of sarcasm and fond familiarity.

"You coppers can debate all you want, but you won't get it right until you conclude that *I* make the best Irish coffee in the world—maybe even the known and unknown universe. And let me tell ya again, sweet lips, old Charlie knows how to do it just right for ya." He waggled his bushy brows at Kait.

"I'm totally on Team C!" Kait raised her hands in surrender. "I concede that your Irish coffee skills are so vast that you make my very queer heart go pitter-patter like no man ever will."

"That makes my day, sweet lips," Charlie said with a wink.

Dean chuckled, shaking his head. "I still don't know why she's let you live this long calling her that."

"She lets me live because our relationship is bound by Irish whiskey."

"That's right, C, baby. And Irish whiskey is stronger than mother's milk—or so my Irish granddaddy tells me. And sometimes looking forward to your Irish coffee is all that gets me through our night shifts in this magnificent, batshit-crazy city." Kait laughed.

Charlie leaned over the bar to scoop up the cash Dean plunked down between them. "You know you coppers don't have to pay." He winked at Kait again. "Especially you, sweet lips."

"But you know we always do," Dean said. "You ready to go?" he asked his partner.

Pulling a dog-eared copy of *We Were Feminists Once* from her vegan leather satchel, Kait shook her head. "Nope, it's my Friday. I'm staying. Going to get some reading done. In peace. You should, too, after what you saw. Well, you drink and I'll read." She caught Charlie's eye. "Another for me, C, and I'm moving over there to my spot by the window. You joining me?"

"Nah, I'm beat, and you know that German *shedder* of yours will still be waiting, leash in mouth, for her walk no matter when you get home," Dean said.

"I know that, which is why I'm going to have another drink here, *in peace*, before I go home to that shedding Nazi. And I know damn well you aren't heading home yet either, no matter how beat you are."

"Gotta count 'em." Dean grinned at his partner. He liked that they knew each other so well they could predict each other's behavior. It felt good. Felt like family. Hell, better than family because they'd chosen each other.

"Counting the crazy swimming people will not *actually* keep them safe," Kait said, laughing, as she settled into her booth, book in hand.

"Okay, I'll concede that the counting of the lap swimmers may be a little obsessive, if you'll concede that, with me watching, it's less possible that accidents will happen to them."

"Dean, you're a crappy swimmer," Kait said.

"No, I'm a strong swimmer. I just hate the water. There's a difference."

"Fine, fine—I'll concede as long as you don't tell the German that I'm avoiding her walk. You know how she gets."

"Deal. See you in a couple days. Unless you want to jog with me tomorrow?"

"Uh, hell no. Jogging sucks worse than hot yoga, which is why I choose hot yoga. Want to skip the destruction of your knees and join me instead?"

"To quote a genius, *uh, hell no*. See, the thing about hot yoga is that it is too fucking *hot*. See you Wednesday night!" Dean's wave took in Kait, Charlie, and the rest of the bar. The regulars waved back and called their goodbyes. Dean exited on a tide of warmth and familiarity, which only made the brisk bay breeze seem even colder than usual. "Summer in SF is TFF—too fucking frigid. But I'll bet this month's pay there are a bunch of crazy swimming people in the bay," he muttered as he shivered and zipped up his leather jacket.

Dean kicked into a quick jog to cross Beach Street, dodging an early morning trolley car, and then cut across quaint Aquatic Park, heading for the nearby Hyde Street Pier. It was only a little past 8:30 A.M., but already the walkway following the half-moon beach was busy with joggers and dog walkers. There was even an elderly T-shirt vendor beginning to set up his wares.

"*Ohayou gozaimasu*, Officer Kent-san. Off to make your count?"

Dean nodded and smiled at the old man. "*Ohayou*, Hikaru. Yep, just keeping it safe out there."

"You know, you may be more superstitious than my old Baba—and that takes some doing," said Hikaru.

"Baba—that's 'grandmother,' right?"

"*Hai!*" Hikaru smiled and nodded. "You're doing well with your Japanese lessons."

"I'm too stubborn to let your language defeat me." Dean smiled back at the old man.

"Ah, yes, remember if you fall down seven times—"

"Get up eight." Dean completed the ancient saying.

"Very good, very good." The old man waved Dean away. "Now get on with your count."

Dean followed Hyde Street past the beginnings of San Francisco's unique mixture of touristy shops, restaurants, and busy locals that made up the Fisherman's Wharf area. It was still early enough for it to be fairly empty. He slowed to a stroll as he passed under the arch that proclaimed HYDE ST. PIER in big, block letters. Picking a spot just astern of the *Balclutha,* a meticulously restored old square-sailed ship that was now a floating museum, Dean leaned on the dock rail, focused on the section of the bay known as Aquatic Park Cove, and began his count.

"One, two, three, four, five, six, seven, eight, nine, ten, eleven," he rattled off quickly under his breath. Dean's eyes searched the morning water. "Twelve," he began, and then frowned. "Cancel that—it's a sea lion. So, eleven crazies. Big number, even for a Sunday morning. Maybe they didn't get the memo that it's fifty fucking degrees out." He studied the swimmers, shaking his head with the mixture of curiosity and confusion they always evoked in him. "Huh, looks like several of them are women. Now that *is* crazy. As Kait would say, women usually have more sense than that." A seagull landed near him and made a scolding sound. "What? They can't hear me. Plus, they gotta know they're crazy." *Or maybe I'm the crazy one. I'm out here in the cold counting swimmers*

27

when I could be inside with Kait counting Irish coffees. Why the hell do I think counting them will keep them safe?

But Dean knew the answer, though he didn't speak it or the question aloud. He could still hear the echo of his father's voice in his memory—he could still see that dark blue uniform and the wide black braid that had stretched proudly down the length of his father's SFPD uniform. *Going to count it out, son. Going to count out all the stores and restaurants and blocks on my beat. Going to count them out to keep them safe.*

It hadn't worked for his father, but somehow the counting had stuck with Dean, and morphed into the crazy swimmer count. So far, it'd worked for him. So far.

Dean shook himself. No. Dark thoughts had no place in this bright, beautiful morning. Scanning from the cove to the dock, Dean walked slowly past the *Balclutha*, making his way to the end of the pier.

Alcatraz was there, sitting in the middle of the bay like a roughly hewn ocean jewel. Though he'd been born and raised within a five-mile radius of Fisherman's Wharf, Dean had never visited Alcatraz. He understood the public's fascination with the island—it was a piece of living history. It was also a prison. Dean was thinking of the tide of tourists that flowed through The Rock every day when movement in the water just a few yards off the end of the pier caught his eye.

Dean focused on the lapping cerulean waves, expecting to see the slick, brown head of another sea lion. Instead, a curtain of strawberry blonde hair fanned around a floating body. Dean blinked hard and squinted. The curtain of hair lifted, and for an instant he saw alabaster skin. The body

seemed to spasm—he was sure he heard a gagging cough—
just before it relaxed back down into the water.

"SFPD! Call 911!" Dean shouted at a fisherman who
was lazily casting a line not far up the pier. He ripped off his
jacket, kicked off his boots, and, with zero hesitation, dove
into the frigid water.

The cold cut him like a blade. Dean expected it, though.
*Ignore the cold. Concentrate. Get to the vic. Ignore the cold...
ignore the cold...* played over and over in his mind as Dean
stroked against the waves. He lifted his head, taking in air
and blinking salt from his eyes. And he saw her! He battled
the waves, stroking five, six, seven more times.

"Got ya!" Dean snagged her outstretched hand, and
then the water exploded in foam as the body came alive. In a
tangle of hair and spray, she surged away from him, kicking
out with such ferocity that the ball of one of her feet caught
him in his stomach.

"Stop! Let me go!"

Too busy trying to gulp for air while he kept a grip on
her wrist, Dean let the young woman pull him with her as
she flailed hysterically and tried to get free.

"Wait!" Dean gasped. "SFPD—I'm here to help."

"Let me go!" she repeated, though she'd stopped kicking
out at him.

"I'll let go if you can show me you're not drowning."
Dean spoke quickly between mouthfuls of seawater.

She immediately stopped struggling. Then she tossed
back her hair and looked Dean fully in the face.

"Drowning? You thought I was drowning?" Her emerald
eyes sparkled with humor.

"Yes, ma'am. You were floating facedown, and then you

were choking. I ascertained that you needed help." Dean reverted to cop speak as he struggled to tread the freezing water and have a conversation with a decidedly *not* drowning woman who looked like a sea goddess.

"Oh, no. I'm sorry for the confusion." She paused and glanced down at his clothes. "I'm also sorry you got all wet. It's sweet that you thought to save me, though. From *drowning!*" As she repeated the word, her voice broke into musical laughter lovelier than anything Dean had ever heard.

He couldn't speak. All he could do was stare at her and let her laughter play around and over him. The sound of it seemed to wrap him in warmth and light, making his blood pound hot through his body, chasing away the cold of the water—the scent of salt and sand—the sounds of seabirds and sea lions—everything, *everything* except her, the sea goddess. That smile! It blazed with happiness and life and sex—definitely sex.

Dean still had hold of her wrist. Almost without willing it, he began to pull, guiding her toward him as her laughter shimmered around them.

"MELODY, COME!"

The shout was a clarion call that shattered the spell between them. She jerked her wrist from Dean's grip and began to swim past him.

"Hang on!" he called, and somehow managed to keep up with her. "Don't go," Dean shouted. "Not yet! Is that you? Is Melody your name?"

With a litheness that made the bay's graceful sea lions seem old and tired, she spun in the water to face him, somehow lifting herself up so that her hair spread around her like an erotic veil, just diaphanous enough to reveal the skin-hugging, jade-green wetsuit covering her body, displaying curves that had Dean's blood pounding so hard that he was starting to feel dizzy.

"Wh—what are you?" he stuttered.

"*There's no one here; you don't want to be here.*" She spoke slowly, rhythmically, almost as if she were singing. "*There's no one here; you don't want to be here.*"

Dean spit out a mouthful of saltwater before responding. "Yeah, I don't want to be out here, in this freezing water, fully dressed. So, uh, how about getting a cup of nice, hot coffee?"

She frowned. Her body sank down into the waves, so that she, once again, gracefully treaded water. "I said, *there's no one here; you don't want to be here.*"

"I heard you. So let's get out of here and get a cup of coffee."

Her frown deepened so that her smooth brow furrowed. "It isn't working."

Dean tried to shrug, and another wave smacked him in the face, making him sputter and sound like he was the one who needed saving. "Sorry, ma'am. I—I'm not trying to be inappropriate. Damn, this is awkward. I'm Dean Kent, and I'm a police officer—part of the San Francisco Police Department, the SFPD. How about I help you back to shore—no strings attached."

She looked around as if checking for strings before saying, "That is kind of you, but as I said, I can't drown, so I don't need any help. And my, um, friends are missing me. Thank you for wanting to save me." She started to swim away again, and Dean stroked forward, grabbing her ankle.

This time when she spun around, her hair flew about her, making her look like an avenging mermaid. "Let me go!"

Dean dropped her ankle. "Sorry—sorry. You didn't tell me your name."

She met his gaze. Rising up out of the water, she said in the same, singsong voice as before, "*You don't want to know my name; there's no one here; you don't want to be here.*"

It was Dean's turn to frown. "Hey, I get it. I'm sure I'm coming off as a real perv. I'm not, though. I'm really a cop. Uh, and not a pervy one."

In the distance sirens began to echo off the water. From the pier, the fisherman cupped his hands around his mouth and shouted, "Hang on, officer! EMTs are coming!"

Dean pointed toward the shore. "Told you I'm a cop!"

"Police? The authorities?"

He nodded, still smiling. "Yep, totally aboveboard. One of the good guys. Promise. Now, will you tell me your name and let me help you out of this freezing mess?"

"You can call me Mel." Her smile flashed for an instant, and then she disappeared under the water, only to reappear a few heartbeats later, already yards from him, swimming with such strength and speed that she left him behind easily—making it completely clear that she had never, not for an instant, needed saving.

CHAPTER FOUR

Tourists traipsed down Beach Street, taking in the expanse of posters and pamphlets advertising "Award-Winning Siren Boat Tours to Alcatraz!" Melody huffed, and busied herself with tidying up the nearest display whenever eyes settled on her. She knew from the orientation she'd suffered through the night before that she was supposed to be perky and helpful when the hordes passed by, but she couldn't muster the enthusiasm.

Pebbles of anxiety collected within her chest, expanding into suffocating boulders when she thought about her swim to the Mortal Realm—that strange, dark creature and that frightened voice.

"No, you're not going to think about that." She shook her head, driving away the memory. "And you definitely can't say anything to anyone. The other girls already think you're weird enough. Sharing this wouldn't help." She sighed. "You were just scared and seeing things, but you made it here. Everything is fine."

Isn't it?

"Ugh. Stop it, Melody," she scolded. "Think about something else." Finished reorganizing the souvenir magnets for the hundredth time, Melody lazily shuffled to the checkout counter at the back of the store. Framed pictures of happy tourists waving and giving thumbs-ups hung from the exposed-brick walls around a poster-sized image of a gaggle of sightseers leaning over a Siren Tours boat, pointing at a fat, speckled sea lion poking its head out of the water curiously. It looked a lot like the one she'd seen yesterday, right before that man scared it away.

"*Mel.* Ugh. Why would I ever tell anyone to call me Mel? It's not even an entire name." The frantic, panicked feeling returned to her chest. Her stomach clenched, and she heaved forward over the countertop. Puffs of fog invaded the outer rim of her vision before taking over completely.

Mel, you are the most amazing person I've ever known.

Red petals flickered on the floor; there, then gone and back again just as quickly. She gripped the lip of the counter, forcing herself to hold on to what she knew was real.

I would be honored to spend the rest of my life with you.

The specter of a kneeling man flashed with the rose petals. She squinted. His features were blurry, but she could make out a small black box resting in his open palm.

Marry me. Make me the happiest man in the world.

Joy flooded her chest, shining through the dark cloud of fear stifling her breath.

She laughed, immediately clapping her hand over her mouth. That sound didn't belong to her. Neither did the excitement, or the flowers, or the ghost of a man.

What was happening?

"You know, friendliness is one of the amazing qualities Siren Tours is famous for possessing," Harmony chided, emerging from the tiny office tucked back in the corner behind the front desk.

Melody exhaled a forceful, quivering breath.

"Didn't mean to scare you." Harmony's sun-streaked curls brushed against Melody's bare shoulder as she came to stand beside her. "Everything okay?"

No! Help me! The terrified exclamations rested on her tongue. "I'm fine." She peered down at the darkened screen of the iPad used to make sales and book tours. The mask of foundation, bronzer, and blush startled her, and she did a quick double take. The makeup she had to wear to hide the effects of rapid aging her kind was cursed with made her skin hot and itchy.

"No, you're not fine. Sometimes I think you forget I practically raised you. Also, you're not a very good liar." Harmony smiled her persuasive smile. "Tell me what's going on."

Melody averted her eyes from Harmony's probing stare and looked out the store's giant picture window and over the ocean. Goose bumps popped up on her tingling flesh as she fought the urge to race to the beach, strip off her street clothes, and dive into the nurturing waves. "My voice—it's…part of me is broken." She didn't dare mention the strange, flickering images or the fearful voice she'd heard in the water. Not until she knew more.

Harmony placed her hand on Melody's shoulder and patted it gently. "Coming to the Mortal Realm is always difficult. More so for you because of what happened to Melisma." She paused. "But that doesn't mean you're broken."

"I met someone yesterday. A man," she blurted, unsure of how best to fill Harmony in on her awkward exchange. "Well, kind of met. I more just tried to get away." She shook her head. "Anyway, when I told him he didn't want to be there, he didn't hear me."

Confusion furrowed Harmony's brow.

"I mean, he heard me, but he didn't *hear me* hear me."

Harmony's eyes widened. "Oh! Well, you hadn't used the ability before. What you need is practice." She trotted out the front of the store and stood on the sun-soaked sidewalk. Her snug top was tucked into a pair of stonewashed bellbottoms that brushed against the top of her pointed heels as she moved. She spotted someone and flapped her hands, motioning for Melody to come over.

She grimaced and stared down at her bare feet. Sparkling lime nail polish winked up at her, and she wiggled her toes before slipping them into her flats.

"Sam, this is Melody, one of the many beautiful tour guides who work with us."

He nodded politely, the freckles speckling his forehead shifting as he lifted his brow.

"I was just telling Sam that we have the best tour boats around, and the most fantastic group of ladies onboard. Maybe you can tell him a little bit more about the packages we offer, and see if you can talk him into joining a group this afternoon." She nudged Melody with her elbow and winked.

"Oh, yes. Let's see. A boat leaves every thirty minutes from Pier 33, and—"

"Wait, I'm sorry to stop you, but I really don't have any time today and I leave town tomorrow." A soft breeze blew in from the bay, puffing his mop of dark curls. "How about

I grab one of your brochures, and next time I'm in the area, I'll come by and set something up?" He stepped up to the carousel of tour information and plucked a pamphlet off the rack.

"Yeah, okay. Sure. That sounds good." Melody feigned enthusiasm.

Harmony leaned into Melody, her voice a gravelly whisper. "Try harder. Do not let him leave without doing what you ask."

Fueled with determination, she stomped toward him. "Sam! One more thing before you go." A knot of uncertainty tightened within her throat, and she swallowed hard. *"Whatever else you have planned today doesn't matter. You want to go on this tour, and you want to go now."*

He chuckled. "Wait, are you serious?" His glance ping-ponged between the two women.

"Very." Melody balled her hands and tried again. *"You want to do this more than you've wanted anything."*

"I can't believe this technique really works for you." He stuffed the brochure back into the rack. "You people are crazy, and I'll be sure to make note of that when I leave a review on Trip Advisor."

Harmony darted next to Melody. Hot spikes of energy shot off of her. *"You were never here. Cross the street, go on with your day, and have a lovely afternoon."*

Sam's eyes glazed over, and his shoulders sagged in relaxation. "I was never here. I'm going to cross the street and go on with my day," he repeated, a grin lifting his cheeks as he stared at Melody. No, *through* Melody. "The afternoon is lovely, isn't it?" He nodded to himself, checked the street for traffic, and jogged toward the park.

Melody shielded her eyes against the sun and watched Sam head to the pier, a slight bounce in his step. "You're really good at that."

"Do it enough and it's as easy as breathing. You'll get the hang of it."

Melody dropped her hand and faced Harmony. "It didn't look like he even saw me anymore. It was like I'd disappeared."

"You had. To him, anyway. What human men see, the decisions they think they're making on their own, it's all too easy to mess with. But you shouldn't do it often, and definitely not over and over again to the same person."

"So I don't hurt someone?" She shifted nervously. She shouldn't care about hurting a human. Especially not a man.

Harmony shrugged. "I guess. It's really so you don't arouse suspicion."

The breeze picked up as it rolled in off the ocean. Melody breathed in the crisp, salty air. "So it's not true, then? That there's something wrong with me."

"Don't worry. You're fine. It takes some Sirens longer, that's all. But you will have to practice. The ability to control what men do, think, and say is extremely important and plays a major role in our purpose here."

Melody folded her arms in front of her chest and stiffened against the dread hardening within her. "To find someone to have sex with, then kill."

"Keep your voice down!" Harmony hissed. "But evidence cleanup is something I always look forward to." Her eyebrow arched and a sly grin curled her lips. "Men taste *so* good."

Melody's stomach roiled even though she knew she

should feel that same excited, murderous hunger. She let out a slow breath. "Yeah, yummy." A bottle cap rested near her foot, and she kicked it with the toe of her shoe. Lazily, it tripped off the curb and vanished down the storm drain. She wished she could squeeze between the teeth of the drain and disappear under the city. She wasn't ready to be a killer. A part of her hoped she never would be.

"So you have to practice, focus, and know you can do it," Harmony continued. "An important thing to ask yourself is whether or not you believe you'll be able to uncover your ability. So, the question really is, do *you* think you'll be fine?"

Up the street, tourists disappeared inside the Franklin Bowles art gallery, and Melody's attention shifted to a new specimen. As he stretched his arms overhead, his T-shirt lifted, revealing a sliver of his toned stomach. He looked familiar, kind of like the man she'd just mentioned to Harmony. What was his name? Doug? Dan? No, *Dean*. Dean had been cute in the water, drenched and wide-eyed like an otter, but this guy was handsome. Chiseled and handsome. She let her gaze wander over him. His hair was unusual. Silver flecks sparkled through the charcoal strands around his temples, but he didn't look old. Not at all. And even from down the street she appreciated the firm line of his jaw and his wide, strong shoulders. Intrigue tickled her chest. He wasn't just handsome. He was—what was it Harmony called it—hott with two *t*'s? Supposedly that meant handsome times ten. He stretched again, showing a little more of his flat abs, and Melody sighed happily.

Like he'd heard her silent praise, he turned toward her, shattering the hott daydream she was creating in her mind.

His shockingly blue eyes met hers. They widened in happy surprise.

Dean?

She looked away hastily.

"No. Oh, no." Melody retreated into the store, pulled the door closed, and pressed herself against the brick wall.

Harmony opened the door with a huff. "There's no reason to be so dramatic. We all go through it."

"No, it's not that. It's *him*." She slid down the wall and dropped her forehead against her knees. "I thought the Mortal Realm was too big for this."

"Sam? That's not possible. I just got rid of him." Harmony propped open the door and poked her head outside.

"It's not Sam, it's Dean. The guy from yesterday." She groaned.

"Ooooh." Harmony stepped inside and busied herself straightening T-shirts that didn't need straightening.

"Ooooh?" Melody lifted her head. "What do you mean, *ooooh*? I need your help. Stand in front of me so I can hide behind you."

Harmony shook her head, her stormy eyes brightening as she chuckled. "You need to meet a man, and this man may actually want to talk with you. Be grateful." Her brow furrowed. "And stop crouching in the corner."

"What are you talking about?" She crawled over to Harmony, positioning herself behind her before she stood. "He's not actually coming over here, is he?" She peeked out from behind Harmony's mass of thick curls and scanned the pedestrians.

"Of course he's coming over here. You're beautiful and

desirable—everything a Siren should be. Now, relax and smile. I'll do the rest."

"No, I can't—" Melody began, but the bell above the door interrupted her.

Smiling, Dean stepped into the store.

CHAPTER FIVE

Dean loved his condo. He'd hardly believed his luck the year before when the building that had been a crumbling fire hazard beside the Buena Vista bar was bought by his Nana's old college roommate and renovated into slick lofts—*and* he'd been invited to move in, with rent control, as long as he promised to be seen in his SFPD uniform. A lot. Dean jumped at the chance to live opposite Fisherman's Wharf, waking up every day to what he considered to be the best view in San Francisco.

"Gotta remember to call Nana and see if she wants to go out to dinner this week," Dean mumbled to himself as he trotted down the stairs, taking them two at a time.

"Good afternoon, Officer Kent. Or I suppose I should say good morning." The man closed his mailbox and leaned against the row of gold postboxes before continuing, "Are you ever going to get off that wretched night shift and join the living?"

Dean chuckled at his neighbor. "Hi there, Stephan. You

know I like the night shift—it keeps life interesting. Hey, nice shirt."

Stephan shifted his handful of mail and tossed back his sparkly gold lamé headscarf as if it were a mane of hair. He batted big, brown eyes at Dean, lashes fluttering flirtatiously. "Boyfriend, are you one hundred percent positive you're not just a tiny bit gay? You always notice my T-shirts, which is not usually a hetero guy thing."

"It might not be a hetero guy thing, but paying attention to details is definitely a cop thing. Plus, I'm a Superman fan." Dean pointed to Stephan's shirt, which read CLARK KENT WAS VEGAN in big, bold letters.

"Well, if you decide to give dick a try, promise I'll be the first to know about it."

"I promise." Dean squinted out the glass front door of the condo complex and then gasped in mock horror. "What is that yellow ball of fire in the sky? The sun? In the summer? In San Francisco?"

"Yaaasss, honey. And in the late afternoon, too. Not even a hint of fog today and it might be almost sixty-five degrees out there. Lucky you if it's your day off," Stephan said.

"It is! Damn, I've never been so glad I couldn't sleep."

"Trouble sleeping? I could help you with that." Stephan's grin was that of a cat licking cream.

"I'll take it if the *help* is a redhead named Mel."

"A ginge? Really? No wonder you couldn't sleep. She's probably already started to suck out your soul."

Dean laughed. "Just because she has red hair doesn't mean she's soulless."

"Oh, you sweet, deluded boy. I'll light a candle for you."

Stephan squeezed Dean's shoulder in mock sympathy before flitting featherlike up the stairs.

Still chuckling, Dean stepped out onto the stoop of the brick building, faced the sun, and stretched mightily. Shit, he was stiff! The impromptu swim he'd taken that morning had made his muscles ache.

But he didn't for one moment regret that he'd jumped into that crazy-cold water, because he'd met *her*. Mel. Her green eyes and alabaster skin haunted his sleep, and her curves filled the brief, intense dreams he'd had, finally waking him, hot and hard, and definitely unfulfilled.

He needed to find her.

Okay, so, he was a cop. It couldn't be that tough. She was one of the crazy swimming people. From watching them for years, one thing he was sure of was that they were all addicted. Once they'd started swimming the cove, they couldn't stay away. Maybe she was back now. This time when he saw her, he damn sure wasn't going to let her get away until he found out her whole name. But first, he needed food.

A giant yawn caught him off guard and he stretched again. The sun felt so good! Almost as if it were the gaze of a beautiful woman—warming him, touching him, wanting him…

Dean rubbed his growling stomach as he looked from the gray waters of the cove up the street toward Lori's Diner. A copper flash drew his eye and he froze in shock.

It was *her*. Mel. She was standing in front of a storefront just a few buildings down. Or, she had been for a heartbeat. The moment their eyes met, she'd whirled away, but Dean was already moving when she disappeared into the store. He jogged down Beach Street, weaving through tourists as he hurried to the shop. He paused for only a second to take in the name of the business—Siren Tours—before opening the door. A bell rang merrily, announcing his arrival.

"Good afternoon! Welcome to Siren Tours."

A tall, pretty blonde waved at him. He meant to wave back—meant to be polite and proper, but as soon as she spoke she stepped aside, revealing the girl who had been standing behind her on the far side of the counter. Dean's world narrowed to her pine-green eyes and her full lips.

"Mel, I thought that was you. I can't believe my luck. I was just thinking about you, and it's like you suddenly appeared."

"Hello."

Her smile was as nervous as it was beautiful. He smiled back at her, doing his best to look nonthreatening and non-stalkerlike.

"How are you? I mean, you swam away so fast I figured you were okay, but that water's pretty rough out there," Dean said.

The blonde's laughter was a bright, happy sound that filled the little store. "Oh, Melody is a strong swimmer. You don't ever need to worry about her in the water."

"Melody," Dean repeated. "That's a lot prettier than Mel."

"Yes," Melody said. "Thank you."

There was an awkward silence during which Dean frantically tried to come up with something, *anything* charming, or at least intelligent, to say. Thankfully, Melody's friend came to his rescue.

"You must be the hero who thought our Melody needed saving yesterday morning." She held out her hand. "I'm Harmony Seirina, Melody's cousin. Thanks for going into the water after her."

"Dean Kent," he said, taking her hand. "It's nice to meet you."

She looked from Dean to Melody, and her gray eyes sparkled mischievously. "Melody, you didn't tell me your hero was so handsome!"

Melody blushed attractively.

"Not surprising. I'm sure I looked like a drowned rat out there with my clothes soaked, insisting your cousin needed saving."

"Dean, I'm sure you exaggerate. No amount of water could possibly tone down all of your yumminess."

"Harmony! You're embarrassing him," Melody said, though Dean noted that now her cheeks were flaming pink.

"Oh, Dean knows I'm just teasing," Harmony said. "Hey, what were you doing out there that made this poor man think you were drowning?"

Melody's eyes met Dean's and her lips lifted in the beginnings of a real smile. "I was laughing."

"You were what?" Dean asked, grinning at her.

"Laughing," she repeated. "I met a fat, round sea lion, and he said the funniest things." Her nose wrinkled with glee.

"A talking sea lion. Wouldn't that have been a sight?" Harmony chuckled awkwardly. "Our Melody makes up the best stories, don't you?"

"Oh. Yeah." The joy slipped from her pink lips. "I was just laughing and swallowed a mouthful of seawater, and that made me cough."

"Ah, that makes sense. I heard you coughing and thought you were drowning." He wanted to bring back that smile. "But I'd like to meet your sea lion friend. He sounds like quite the comedian."

Dean's chest warmed as cheer returned to Melody's cheeks. "I appreciate you jumping in after me. Fully clothed and looking like a drowned rat."

"No problem at all. It's part of my job, though I admit that not saving you was a true pleasure. Although in my head that came out much nicer than it sounds." Dean cleared his throat and took the leap. "So, um, I'm off today and I was wondering if you might like to get a cup of coffee, or a glass of wine, or breakfast—well, my breakfast, probably your dinner. I work nights, so this is really my morning. But I'm up for eating or drinking pretty much anything. With you, I mean." Dean ran a hand through his hair. "Damn, sorry. I don't know what's wrong with me. I don't usually have mouth diarrhea."

Melody frowned, studying him closely. "Mouth diarrhea?"

"No! I didn't mean to say that. I'm usually not this big of an idiot, either. I'm not sure why I'm screwing this up. Probably because you're so damn beautiful that you make it hard for me to think."

Harmony's laughter sparkled around them again. "Oh, Dean, you're not screwing anything up. I think you're charming. Don't you, Melody?"

"I suppose. If you don't really have mouth diarrhea."

Dean's cheeks heated. "I don't. I promise. Listen, I'll prove it. I'll say this fast and to the point. Melody, would you please go out with me?"

"I can't." She shrugged. "I have to work."

Dean's heart was in the process of falling into his gut when Harmony spoke up.

"Oh, Melody, don't be silly. I'm sure you can do both!" she said happily.

"Both?" Melody asked.

"Sure! Dean, Melody *does* have to work, but you could join her today because she's still in training and won't actually be guiding a tour, just observing. Or have you been to Alcatraz too many times for it to still be interesting for you?"

A wave of relief swept over him. "Believe it or not, I've *never* been to Alcatraz."

"Perfect! Then it's settled." Harmony pulled out a roll of fat tickets and ripped one off, handing it to Dean. "There you are, sir. One ticket for Siren Tours' Alcatraz Adventure, which will be personally guided by your very own Siren-in-training, Melody. The ferry departs from Pier 33 in twenty minutes. You two just have time to make it. Have a fabulous afternoon, Dean. Be gentle with her—this is her first time. And *Mel*, don't worry about coming back to the shop. I'll close up tonight."

With strength that surprised Dean, Harmony took him by one arm and Melody by another and propelled them out of the door, closing it firmly behind them.

CHAPTER SIX

Uneasiness quaked within Melody, rattling her teeth. She tensed her jaw to silence their clacking. In twenty-five years, this was her first official date. Having fake encounters with older Sirens pretending to be interested males hadn't been challenging. Actually, it'd been funny to hear such dulcet voices forced into gruff, cracking baritones. Her time in Tartarus had been training. This was the real deal.

"I've noticed these ferries before," Dean said as they settled into a standing place near the bow of the boat. His gesture took in the gorgeous, mostly naked mermaid that was painted along the side of the vessel. "Not the biggest tour boat, but the prettiest by far."

"It's our logo." She relaxed a bit as she spoke. "Though it's a little confusing because it's a mermaid and not a Siren."

"Does it matter?"

She bit her tongue, stopping herself from launching into a lecture on the differences between the two. "Only if you're a mermaid or a Siren." She shrugged.

"Excuse me, sir. May I get you something to drink? Beer or a glass of wine?"

The hairs on the back of Melody's neck stood at attention as she turned to face the familiar voice.

"Oh, Melody! I didn't know you were leading a tour today." Aria flipped her blonde hair and let her hand trace the silhouette of the sexy sailor's outfit that was the Siren Tours uniform.

"I'm not," she said, her jaw again clenched. "I'm just observing."

There was a small silence, which Dean filled by sticking out his hand.

"Hi, I'm Dean Kent—Melody's date."

"Well, *hello there*, Dean Kent. It is soooo nice to meet you. I'm Aria, Melody's cousin." She cocked her hip to the side and studied him. "You *are* a handsome one, aren't you? Good job, Mel—"

"Aria!" She barked the name. "The man in the red jacket way over there by the stern is trying to wave you down. He looks thirsty."

Melody's stomach tumbled just as it had in the shop, with the rose petals and that man.

Don't let them have him.

Had that thought been her own? The voice was deeper, richer, different than hers.

"Well, poo!" Aria pouted. "You're keeping this handsome man all to yourself?"

"Yes." She grabbed Aria by the elbow and led her away from Dean. "He is *my* date. You and the rest of the girls need to understand that. You *can't* have him."

"All right, all right," she grumbled, shaking her arm away from Melody's grasp. "You never have liked to share."

"And you'll tell the others?"

"Yes." She sounded exasperated. "Stop freaking out. I'll tell the girls onboard that he's off-limits." She paused for a moment, seeming to size up the young Siren. "Coming up here has really released your inner huntress. You should be proud." With a wave, she sauntered toward a group of unsuspecting tourists. "See ya later at the condo—unless I get lucky too."

Huntress? Melody stuffed her hands into her pockets and took a cleansing breath before returning to Dean.

"Another cousin?" he asked as she approached.

"Yeah, sorry about that." She leaned into the railing, comforted by the mist of seawater dusting her face. "I'm not good at this dating thing. I'm especially not good at it when my cousins are lurking around ready to pounce on you if I mess up."

Dean shook his head. "Hey, you're not messing up, and I don't care how many gorgeous cousins you have lurking around here. It's you I'm interested in." He waited a beat and then added, "How many gorgeous cousins do you have, anyway?"

"More than I wish I had." She thought back to the crowded pool in Tartarus that felt so safe, but that was now so far away. "You'll see when we get to Alcatraz."

"Oh, I get it! This is a family business." Dean scooted closer and rested his forearms on the white railing. Melody yearned to be that relaxed. She took her hands out of her pockets and mirrored his posture.

"Yes, exactly," she said, watching their reflections quiver in the waves.

"I'm in the family business too," he said.

She cocked her head to the side, looking over at him. "The police are your family? You mean literally?"

"Yeah." The lightness fell from his voice. "My dad wore the SFPD uniform for upwards of twenty years, working out of North Station. That's my station now, too."

"That must feel good—working with your father," Melody mused.

"He, uh, he's not with us anymore." His silver-flecked temples pulsed. "But it does feel good to work out of his old station."

Melody didn't know what to say, so she stayed silent.

He pulled his palm over his stubbly chin and swallowed hard. "So, your family owns Siren Tours?"

She nodded. "We all take turns working here."

"You must have a big family," Dean said, the pep returning to his tone.

"You have no idea, though most of us are still back home."

"Back home? Where's that?"

"Tar—" She snapped her mouth shut and stiffened. She'd gotten too comfortable. "Greece," she corrected.

"Greece? That's awesome. Where in Greece?"

"Just a small village by a little cove." She waved her hand dismissively. "I'm sure you've never heard of it."

"Well, I've never been to Greece, but I do have the Internet, and I'll bet it's heard of your little cove. Don't tell anyone, but I am something of a Google Master." He smirked.

Melody forced out a dry chuckle. "Is it okay if we don't talk about my family? Or at least my family back in, uh, Greece. Leaving was hard, and sometimes I miss home so much I feel like I'm going to suffocate, but sometimes I think I'll suffocate if I have to go back."

She picked nervously at her fingernails, and Dean covered her hand gently with his. "Hey, no worries. I get it. Talking about my family can be tough for me, too." He squeezed her hand, and she welcomed the warmth it provided. "And now we have two things in common."

"Two?" A sudden gust blew her hair in front of her face, and she pulled her hands from Dean's to rearrange the tangled tresses.

"Yep, we're both in our family's business, and we can both swim."

"Swim?" Her eyebrows arched. "Is that what you were doing? I thought you might have been on the verge of needing to be saved."

"Hey, I can swim fine." His chest puffed a little as he smoothed out the front of his shirt. "I just don't like the water."

"Don't like the water?" She couldn't contain her burst of giggles.

"It's not funny," Dean grumbled, a dimple forming at the corner of his mouth as his lips quirked up. "But look at it! It's dangerous out there. And cold. And wet. Really wet."

"Of course it's wet. It's the ocean. It's supposed to be wet!" Her cheeks ached with glee. She hadn't laughed that hard in a long time. "And it's only dangerous if you don't understand it." Her gesture took in the tumultuous water of the bay around them. "It's like music."

"Okay, this I have to hear. How could the ocean be like music?" Dean settled back against the railing.

"Imagine the water is an orchestra and each current is a note being played. The waves are voices, singing a tune that changes with the tide. If you can hear its music, you know how to harmonize with it. Do that and the sea will never hurt you. It will only wrap around you and sing your favorite songs."

She paused, waiting for him to say something to quell the embarrassment pricking hot under her skin.

"That must have sounded really silly." She shifted nervously.

"Not at all," he assured her. "It made perfect sense. Unfortunately, I am tone-deaf to the ocean music. But I do finally understand the crazy swimming people."

"Crazy swimming people?" She crossed her arms in front of her chest.

"That's just what I named the people who swim laps in the cove. Now I understand that they might not actually be crazy. They just hear the ocean music. Thanks for clearing that up for me."

"You're welcome. I think." She chewed her lower lip. "Wait, wasn't I one of those crazy swimming people?"

"No!" He straightened his arms, pushing himself off of the balustrade. "I mean, yes. You were one of the swimming people. I'm sorry. I didn't mean to be insulting." His apology seemed genuine. "Your ocean analogy was perfect, even if I don't really understand it. Hey, maybe I'd get it if I went swimming with you."

Her lips twisted in a wry grin. "We've already gone swimming together, Officer Dean."

A woman's canorous voice came from the loudspeaker, interrupting the beginnings of Melody's flirtation. "All passengers please depart our vessel carefully off the starboard side and make your way to our Siren, the beautiful Viola, who is beckoning to you from in front of the gift store area. She will explain the rules of the tour, and then you will be free to explore on your own, or to have a more intimate Alcatraz experience with our special audio tour. Our ferries returning to Pier 33 leave every thirty minutes from right here until 9:00 P.M., when the island closes. Have a wonderful trip, and remember to book Siren Tours next time you're in San Francisco."

"Come on." Melody grabbed the crook of Dean's arm and pulled him toward the exit. "You don't have to listen to the rules—you're with me."

• • •

Dean was happy to let Melody take his arm and practically drag him past the group of eager tourists who were gathering around what looked to be another stunning woman.

"Another cousin?"

"Of course," Melody said. "Okay, like Harmony said, this is my first time on the island too, but I've studied the maps and the general information already. See that really steep walkway that winds up the side of that hill?"

"I do."

"That's where we're going. Up to the prison."

As if she'd just realized she was holding on to him, Melody tried to jerk away from his grasp, but Dean smiled and tucked her hand intimately into his elbow. "By the look of that incline I'm going to need to keep ahold of you."

She placed her free hand on her hip. "Officer Dean, I assure you that I won't have any problem making that hike."

"It's not you I'm worried about." He drew her in closer. "I'm going to hang on to you and pretend like you're not pulling me up that hill."

They trudged up the steep, winding path, stopping for just a moment to gawk, Dean with gruesome fascination and Melody with obvious revulsion, at the small, dingy morgue. Then they headed into the massive prison.

A raw, core-biting chill seeped through his jacket when they stepped inside. Dean tensed against his instinct to leave. Suppressing his misgivings, he forced himself to take in one of his city's top tourist destinations.

"So, this is what everyone comes to see," he murmured, feeling hope drain away as he studied the weathered building that stood hollow and cold like a shadow.

Melody gathered her tousled mane in a tight ponytail and checked the overhead signage. "It's this way," she said, her slight frame easily slipping past the crowd. He fought his way through, following her bouncing copper ponytail.

"Whoops. Sorry about that. Didn't mean to step on your foot!" Dean turned and waved apologetically to the teen he'd nearly trampled. He continued forward, examining the short, narrow cells lining the cellblock. "Oof!" Dean ran smack into Melody, her bent elbow jabbing him in the stomach.

"Sorry," she whispered, her focus never straying from the cluster of three cells, each of which had a dummy head half hidden in its tiny cot.

"That's creepy," he said, massaging the dull ache from

their collision. When Melody remained silent he leaned into her. "Do you know what happened?"

"Oh, yes. Sorry. *Again*." She simpered. "This is where Frank Lee Morris and two brothers, Clarence and John, used spoons to dig around the air vents. That's how they got out."

Dean peered into the cell in front of them. "Where'd they go after they got out?"

Melody motioned for him to follow her to the end of the row, where there was a glass door through which he could see a long utility hallway between the two cellblocks.

"They climbed up one of those iron drainage pipes to the roof." She pressed her index finger against the glass. Her delicate hand made a stark contrast to the thick, rusted metal cluttering the narrow passageway. "Then they made their way to the dining hall and hospital wing, which is where they used a stovepipe to climb down to the water." Melody's voice faded softer and softer until he strained to hear her.

"Then what happened?"

She turned and lifted her chin toward the dingy windows lining the top of the cement wall. "No one knows for sure. The official word is they drowned."

"Would you rather know they were out there, free?"

She shrugged.

Dean shook his head. His inner cop twitched with frustration. "Funny how people forget that they were locked up here because they were violent criminals."

"The whole thing is just so..." She glanced back at the tiny cells. "Awful. So much more awful than I thought it'd be." The depth of sadness in her voice surprised him.

"Are you okay?"

"Yes. No," she whispered, her eyes awash in unshed tears. "Can we get out of here?"

"Of course." This time he took the lead, wrapping Melody's arm protectively through his and guiding her out of the building. Bathed in sunlight once again, she gulped in big breaths of sea air, rubbing her arms while staring out at the bay.

"Hey, what I said back there, it's not that big of a deal. I get wanting to forget the bad and think everything turned out okay."

She shook her head. "It's not that. Didn't you feel it?"

"It?"

"The sadness. The hatred. The horror of it all. I—I didn't realize it would linger. No one told me. None of them—not one of my cousins. They didn't say anything to me." She sighed. "But I don't know what I expected. It was a prison, and prisons are traps, with cages and rules and anger and loneliness," she said, perilously close to tears. "I don't like this place. At all."

Dean wrapped his arms around her, drawing her carefully to him. "Yeah, I felt it." She shuddered and his embrace tightened. "Would you like to leave?"

"Yes." She nodded against his chest. "I'm sorry this is such a bad date."

"Are you kidding? I've got you in my arms already, which means I'm having a great time!"

She leaned back and met his gaze. "Really?"

"Really. And I have the perfect way to make all of that"—he jerked his chin at the hulking building behind them—"all better."

"How?"

"Pasta."

She smiled tentatively. "You mean food."

"I mean a very particular type of food. Italian. Pasta. With lots of bread and olive oil, garlic, and wine."

Melody tilted her head back and Dean became lost in her eyes. So lost that he almost bent and covered those seductive lips with his own. He yearned to taste her—to touch more and more of her—and, surprisingly, to be sure she never looked as afraid and sad as she had just moments ago.

"Pasta is perfect." She beamed.

Using every bit of his self-control, he stepped back, letting his arms slide from around her. "Then let's go eat pasta and drink too much wine," he said, lifting her palm to his lips.

CHAPTER SEVEN

Melody was sure her eyes would pop out of her head before she finished reading Pompeii's Grotto's expansive menu. She flipped through the pages and glanced up at Dean. The corners of his eyes creased with a warm grin. On the boat, she'd felt the need to protect him. It was so fierce she would've carried him overboard and swum to shore before leaving him there alone. She knew what the Sirens would do if given the chance. Dean would be their next victim. Their next meal. Her stomach churned.

Don't let them have him.

"Anything sound good?"

Startled, she shook her head quickly. "I haven't looked yet. Sorry." She flipped back to the first page of entrees. "Seafood," she whispered. Yearning for a plate of salty kelp, or a bowl brimming with seaweed, her stomach growled in response as she perused the options. *Pan-seared scallops.* Her eyes again flicked up to Dean, who was calmly studying the back of the menu. She shrugged, and continued reading. *Grilled jumbo lobster tail.* She wrinkled her nose in disgust.

Melody had been taught that humans ate a wide variety of foods, but that lesson was one of the boring ones she hadn't paid much attention to. But *seafood.* Surely people didn't think sea creatures swam around waiting to be eaten. Maybe this was some sort of test. Melody craned her neck to see if she could spot Harmony or another one of her sisters lurking in the restaurant.

"Something wrong?" Dean's brow crinkled.

"You're not going to eat any seafood, are you?" she blurted.

"Wasn't planning on it. I'm more of a pasta pomodoro guy, and this restaurant makes a great sauce. They call it the Angelina."

Melody exhaled and relaxed against the curved back of the chair. "Good. I've never met a crab who'd agree to be made into a salad, or a clam who chose to be chowder, and I don't understand how they convinced a squid to want to be fried, but here they all are." She released a puff of air and set the closed menu on the red-and-white checkered tablecloth.

"You're a vegetarian. I didn't mean to offend you by bringing you to a place that serves seafood."

"No, it's fine. I'm not a vegetarian. At least, I'm supposed to eat meat, but I don't. There's just so much…blood." Even the word left a sour taste in her mouth.

Dean's head tilted as he listened intently. Melody's eyes traveled along his jawline to his thick chest, and back up again. Blood coursed through the steadily pulsing vein on the side of his neck. She should want to bite into it. Should crave the moment when she could relax and let her True Form take over completely. Each movement with this man should be calculated, fueled by the desire to climax before tearing into his flesh so the hot, dense, scarlet liquid gushed from between mouthfuls of muscle and skin. *Evidence cleanup.* Or so Harmony called it. But it was so much more. An ancient need to protect themselves by devouring their prey.

She shivered, repulsed.

"Good evening, and thank you for coming in to Pompeii's Grotto."

Relieved for the distraction from her own thoughts, Melody turned her attention to the petite, scratchy-voiced waitress. "Can I start you two off with anything to drink? Any appetizers?"

"I'll let the lady pick our poison this evening." Dean slid the wine list across the table.

"Red," Melody noted.

"So, you'd each like a glass of our house red?" Her bushy eyebrow curved into an arch. "It's a fabulous Chianti."

"Yes. And I will eat the Angelina," Melody said quickly, trying to mask her embarrassment.

"I'll have the same."

"And some of the brussels sprouts," she added.

"You're going to love the Angelina, and not enough people order the brussels sprouts. They are delicious." She collected the menus, and offered a weathered smile before rushing toward the kitchen.

"Brussels sprouts?" Dean cringed, the tiny crease between his eyebrows deepening.

"She said they're delicious. Plus, they're cruciferous." She echoed one of the only facts she remembered about her lesson on food. "That's a funny word when you say it out loud. *Cruciferous*," she enunciated, her laughter twinkling around them.

Dean held her gaze for an uncomfortably long time. His eyes were warm and inviting, two calm pools in the midst of the sea of chaos that was San Francisco. But she didn't like them settled on her, not right now, anyway. Nervously, she grabbed the burgundy napkin off the table and busied herself with unwrapping her silverware.

"I watched *The Little Mermaid* last night. The condo doesn't have very many movie choices," she babbled. "But I didn't understand why Ariel put that fork in her hair. No one does their hair at the dinner table."

Dean chuckled. "Fish can't talk, either, so I think that movie missed the mark on a few levels."

Finally lifting her eyes to meet his, she cocked her head to the side. "Fish *can* talk," she said, whimsy absent from her voice.

The waitress returned, and, with practiced grace, noiselessly placed each glass of wine on its respective cocktail napkin.

"Sure, but not to people," he said after a quick drink.

"Only because people don't know how to listen. Sometimes I wonder how humans have survived for so long, deaf to the world around them." She followed Dean's lead and took a sip of the house red. Bitter liquid spread out over her tongue, and her throat tightened against the thought of swallowing. Covering her mouth with the napkin, she spit out the wine, thankful the fabric matched its hue.

"You're different, you know that?"

Her cheeks blazed.

"That's not a bad thing. I was different for a long time."

He reached across the table and rested his hand on hers. It was warm and heavy and made her skin tingle. "If I tell you something, you promise you won't make fun of me?"

"No." She stifled an excited chortle.

"Fair enough."

Dean released her hand too soon as he made room for two heaping plates of pasta.

"Enjoy," the waitress croaked.

Melody stuck her fork in the middle of the steaming pile and twirled. As the noodles hit her tongue, she closed her eyes and let the newly tasted herbs rest against her palate. "Mmmmm."

"Yep, they know what they're doing back there." Dean nodded toward the swinging kitchen door.

Melody beamed around the satisfying mouthful.

"Okay, you've convinced me. I'm going to let you in on something not too many people know." He let his fork hover above the plate as he spoke. A bright red chunk of tomato slid down the steel and plopped onto the pool of sauce below, splattering damp droplets on his dark shirt. "Hopefully you won't laugh me out of the restaurant."

"Is this a secret?" she asked, leaning over her plate.

"Sure is." He sighed and set down the fork. "All through high school I was the fat kid." He grimaced.

"That doesn't make you sound like you were too different."

"Well, that's not the most embarrassing part." He cleared his throat. "I was a virgin until I was twenty-one. I didn't even have my first kiss until I was about to leave for college."

"Oh," Melody whispered. She'd never been kissed or kissed anyone, and sex for her species always ended in death, so she definitely hadn't done that yet. Until now, she hadn't thought waiting was something to be ashamed of. Her stomach knotted.

"I played football and had friends and everything, but was always looked at as more of a brother to all of the girls. Which sucked if I wanted a date for the movies or a dance, or anywhere at all, really." He fidgeted with his napkin. "So I understand different."

"Well, I think it's great." Melody pushed down her insecurities. "My pace has also been a lot...slower. That shouldn't be a secret. It's nice."

"You're right. I guess it shouldn't be."

Melody let go of the whirlwind of thoughts surrounding her inexperience, and relaxed into the moment.

Patrons came and went, but she and Dean stayed, sharing stories and laughing together for what felt like hours.

"Should we order another one?" He set his fork on the crumb-speckled plate and wiggled his eyebrows encouragingly.

Melody's lip curled at the mischievous twinkle in his eyes. "I want to say yes, but we've already eaten two pieces of cheesecake. We can get another slice next time."

"So you're saying I get to take you out again?"

Her back pocket vibrated for what had to be the hundredth time. "Sorry." She huffed and pulled out her phone. "I have to make sure this isn't an emergency." She opened the ten new texts from Harmony, and scanned them quickly.

Are you still out with him?

You're not answering. That has to mean yes!

How is he?

Ask about his family history.

And remember to RELAX! Your first kill is always the worst. So many nerves!

Melody's stomach dropped. "I need to get home."

"Everything okay?" Concern wrinkled Dean's brow.

"Yeah, it's just late," she lied. "I have to wake up early for work."

"Right. I forget most people's nights aren't their days." His shoulders slumped with the realization. "Should I call you a cab?"

"I can walk." She pushed herself away from the table and stood, collecting her jacket from the back of the chair. "I'm only a couple blocks away, at the Fairmont in Ghirardelli Square."

"Whoa, you must be very successful at Siren Tours to have a residence over there." Dean rounded the table and assisted her while she slipped her arms into the coat's sleeves.

Melody couldn't tell if she was warm because of the added layer, or because of how close Dean's body was to hers. "Harmony worked out a deal with the manager. It's practically free."

Dean pushed in her chair and offered her his arm. "Those are some negotiating skills I wish I had."

"I guess you could say it runs in the family." Melody forced a chuckle, and looped her arm through his.

The sun had been gone for hours, leaving the breeze to cool in its absence. It whipped around them as they strolled down Jefferson Street headed toward the glorious point where water touched land.

Dean stiffened as she pulled him closer to shore.

"What's wrong?" she asked, slipping off her shoes.

He shrugged. "It's cold."

"I'd rather be cold in the water than out." Already having spent too much of the day on dry earth, she charged into the frothy waves, welcoming them as they lapped against her shins. The temptation to give in and allow her ivory skin to morph into its True Form was almost overwhelming. She dug her toes into the sand and clenched her jaw tight as she stared out at the vast black.

"What song is the ocean playing tonight?"

She hadn't heard him splash up next to her, but she welcomed the gentle tide of relaxation he provided. Sinking into the sand, she closed her eyes and let her body feel the music of the abyss. "It's darker, deeper now, the tone of the waves. It's because of the predators. They're hunting and they carry a bass that will shake your bones if you get too close." She opened her eyes, a quiet smile lifting her lips.

Dean stared at her with gentle curiosity. "I like you. A lot. You're so…*free*." He paused. "I think this is the best date I've ever been on."

Melody shook her head. "It can't be. We basically fled Alcatraz *and* dinner, and the bottoms of your pants are soaked."

"Yours are too." He stepped closer to her.

She lifted her foot out of the water and studied her jeans in the glow of the streetlamp. Deep blue reached up from the cuffs, licking just below the knee. Under her foot, the sand shifted as he inched closer.

"But I've been on a lot of first dates." His nose wrinkled. "That sounds wrong. I'm not a serial dater. I've been on a *normal* number of first dates, and this one tops all of those. The rest of them don't even come close, really."

She looked up at him. "You're not joking? Or lying. There are so many lies in this world."

"I won't lie to you." His fingers floated across her forehead, brushing loose strands of copper from in front of her eyes. "That's something my Nana taught me never to do. You'll have to meet her someday."

"Meet Nana?" Excitement raised her onto the balls of her feet. "You would want to take *me* to meet *your* Nana?"

"I didn't say that too soon, did I?"

"I just never thought any man would say anything like that to me." The words left her lips as soft whispers.

"Any man should be honored to have you meet his family. I know I will be—or at least I hope I'll get the chance to be. Say you'll see me again, Melody." His voice deepened and he stepped even closer.

And there were those steel-blue eyes again. On her. Consuming her. Melting away each ugly truth she'd been taught about men. Dean was smart and sweet. He was also brave and strong. He had to be. He was a police officer. From what she remembered from her lessons, police officers were viewed as heroes in the Mortal Realm. Maybe being a human hero made him different from other men.

Dean lifted his hands, gently cupping her face, and Melody stopped breathing as he bent and covered her mouth with his.

The taste of him surprised her. There was wine on his breath as it mingled with hers, but there was something else, something mysterious and alluring. He captivated her, filling her world with his kiss. At first he was gentle. His lips brushed hers and she felt him smile as he murmured, "Your lips are so soft I could kiss you all night."

She opened her mouth to say something, anything, and he claimed her, deepening their kiss so that his tongue began to tease hers.

She'd dreamed about being kissed like this—in the moonlight, standing in the sand with the ocean caressing her feet—but her dreams had only been the fantasies of a girl. They were nothing compared to the reality of this man. His touch, his taste sent shock waves crashing deep within her.

She wanted more. She yearned for more.

Tentatively, Melody returned his kiss, letting her tongue flick against his. The low moan of pleasure that rumbled from Dean encouraged her, and she slid her arms up over his chest to rest on his wide shoulders. His embrace tightened around her, making her insides hum and her skin shudder. She pressed herself to him, dizzy with the cacophony of new feelings the heat of his body thrust against her. Soft, familiar waves cascaded over her skin, pulling her into Dean with almost as much force as she was pulled to the ocean.

His lips left hers and began working their way down the curve of her neck. Melody shivered and opened her eyes. Moonlight glinted off the slick emerald green rippling to life across the arm she'd wrapped around Dean's shoulder.

Panic made her stomach lurch sickeningly.

"Wait, Dean! Please stop." She pushed against his chest, and he took a few steps back to keep from falling. Her body vibrated with the change from skin to scales, and she quickly wrapped her arms tight against her chest. "I'm sorry. I can't. I'm *not* free. I'm not who you think I am. I have to go."

She splashed to shore, and, without grabbing her shoes, tore through Aquatic Park and sprinted to the safety of her San Francisco home.

As she darted through Ghirardelli Square and up the stairs to the back entrance of the Fairmont, she silently reprimanded herself for leaving behind her shoes and Dean without a real explanation.

"He's never going to want to see me again." Tears burned her eyes and she wiped them away quickly, surprised and embarrassed that the thought triggered such a response.

She removed the keycard from her wallet. The lock flashed green and she let out a deep sigh as she walked into the dark apartment.

"That didn't seem to go as planned." The light flicked on and Melody squinted against the sudden change.

She blinked. Harmony stood in the living room, hands on her hips disapprovingly. "You were watching me?"

"I promised your mother I would protect you." They had only been in the Mortal Realm a couple of days, but age was already deepening the lines around Harmony's eyes and mouth. "And it's part of my duty as Caretaker. I have to make sure none of you get caught."

"But you can't spy on all of us all the time. There's only one of you."

"Unless something happens and Rhapsody makes an appearance."

Melody felt around for the couch and collapsed onto it. Waves of heat swirled up from her stomach and rippled through her slowly trembling limbs. "Why, why would she come here?"

"She makes the trip when she thinks one of the girls might cause a problem." Harmony's gaze narrowed.

"Me? I just got here. I'm not causing any problems!"

"I just watched one unfold across the street." Harmony

thrust her finger toward the floor-to-ceiling window behind her. "He clearly wanted you. Why did you run?"

"Because," she whispered. "I'm not like you."

"Melody," Harmony sat down next to her on the couch and squeezed Melody's hand, "I know losing your mother was hard for you; it was for me too. But it's been years. It's time to let go of the past and start a new future. One with a daughter of your own."

A daughter of her own? Her heart fluttered, and her vision hazed as bile surged up her throat.

A dark-haired woman flashed on the couch next to her, filling Harmony's seat, holding her hand just the same.

"No." Melody clutched her stomach as the specter brightened and dimmed just as it had that morning in the store.

Mel, honey, this is so fabulous!

The woman's voice unleashed a pang of longing within Melody's chest.

I knew he would propose soon! I almost burst from keeping the secret. She clapped her translucent hands against her cheeks. Melody stared at her face, blazing in strong flashes against Harmony's. This woman was so familiar.

Now you have to hurry up and have a wedding so you can have a daughter of your own. I can't wait to spoil a grandbaby.

Nausea released its grip, and the otherworldly glimpses faded.

"Next time you see him, you will do what you came here for." Harmony's voice echoed through choppy bursts of reality. "Melody, are you okay?"

The vision was gone, leaving Melody awash in joy and heartbreak. "I can't do what you do."

Don't let them take him.

Backed by another's, her voice was stronger, more confident. "I'm not a monster!"

She tore away from Harmony and dizzily stumbled down the hall to the safety of her room.

A part of her knew that woman. Felt the deep love and the unbreakable connection only attached to a parent. Melody had that devotion to her mom. And now she ached the same way for this ghost of a woman.

She flipped on the bathroom light and filled the sink with cool water. She splashed handfuls on her face before picking up a neatly folded washcloth. She dipped a corner of the cloth in the basin and wiped away the thick layers of makeup suffocating her face. With each pass of the cloth, her skin peeked through, pink with freedom. Her breath caught in her throat as she wiped away the last remaining lines of color. Her fingers traced the smooth, taut skin around her eyes and lips, as she stared into the frightened emerald irises looking back at her.

"What's happening to me?"

CHAPTER EIGHT

Dean tried to hurry after Melody, but the sand seemed to have a life of its own, trapping his feet and sending him to his knees. "I'm fucking soaked *again*, and again she got away from me," he muttered to himself. Streetlights shaped like upside-down teardrops cast enough light that he could track Melody's progress as she sprinted through Aquatic Park. He shuffled to shore and ineffectively wiped at the sand coating his soaked pant legs. When he looked up, she was jogging across Beach Street, and then disappearing into Ghirardelli Square. "Well, at least this time I know where she lives *and* where she works." Determinedly, he bent to pick up both her shoes and his own, and began to follow Melody.

What the hell had happened? Had he been too forceful with her? He hadn't meant to be pushy, but she'd felt so damn good in his arms. And she'd seemed to be enjoying herself. He sighed and shook his head. Maybe it was time he gave in, and listened to what he'd been told all these years— to stop trying to understand women.

"Women," he huffed. "It's like they're a completely different species."

He continued slogging through Aquatic Park, mulling over the knowledge his Nana worked to instill in him. "Find The One, *mio bambino*, and spend your life trying your best to love her." Nana said that was all any man could do. He'd told her that was an old-fashioned way to look at women, but she'd smiled that foxlike grin of hers and said, "Old fashion or old wisdom? Ah, you will see when you finally fall in love."

Dean stopped in the middle of the park like he'd hit a glass wall.

Jesus Christ, am I in love?

Dumbfounded, Dean just stood there, staring at the cream-colored lights that spelled out GHIRARDELLI SQUARE.

"No, not possible. I've only known her for a day." He brushed a sandy hand through his hair. "We've only been out once. Sure it was amazing, and also a little confusing, but it was only one date. It can't happen that fast, can it?"

But there it was—the knot in his gut that he'd never had before. Not when he'd thought he'd fallen in love with Kristi in high school. Not when he'd almost gotten engaged to Adrienne just before he'd graduated from the police academy. Not ever before in his life. The truth was that no woman had ever made him feel the things Melody was making him feel, but whether that meant love or lust, or both, he wasn't sure.

"Well, I'm going to find out."

He kicked into a jog, hurrying to Beach Street, and fidgeted anxiously while a line of empty tour buses crawled past. He cursed, sure that Melody had already reached the

Fairmont, and rushed across the street. He was halfway up the stairs that led to the heart of the square and the posh Fairmont Residences when the huge clock tower began to chime…and chime…and chime.

Midnight wasn't actually late for a date, but *this* date was unusual because they'd been together since early afternoon. First dates never lasted that long! Dean slowed, looking up at the exclusive condos for the rich and famous—and Melody's large extended family. There were some lights on—even some fire pits still burning on private balconies—but what did he think he was going to do, throw rocks at windows hoping to find her?

"Oh, yeah, that'd definitely impress her," he said to himself. No, if he was going to see Melody again, and he was *absolutely* going to see Melody again, he needed a plan. A great one. Heading back to his nearby condo, confidence swelled within him as he pulled out his phone and pressed *Nana*.

"*Buonasera, mio bambino!*" Nana's voice, rich in years and love, answered before there were two rings.

"Hi, Nana," Dean said. "I didn't wake you, did I?"

"Of course not. You know I'm a night owl. I don't trust anyone who goes to bed before midnight. What is it, bambino?"

"I need advice," Dean said.

"Financial or female?"

"The latter."

"*Fantastico!* I'll chill the limoncello glasses. See you in a moment?"

"I'll be there before the glasses are cold."

• • •

Nana was a genius. Or, at least over a bottle of homemade limoncello she'd seemed like a genius. But now, in daylight, and with Dean sober and standing in the middle of a florist shop, he was having second thoughts.

"Officer Dean, you stop that worrying!" The woman who owned Flush Floral patted him absently on the arm.

"Are you sure I chose the right flower? Nana said it was important," Dean said.

"Of course the right flower is important! Your Nana is a wise woman. Okay, once more, tell me why you chose gardenias for your Melody."

"She's not *my* Melody," Dean corrected.

"Not yet maybe, but I have a feeling it's only a matter of time. Now, why gardenias?"

Dean sighed and traced the broad, glossy, dark green leaves of the potted plant. Even through his nerves he had to admit that the fragrance of the white flowers was intoxicating. He just hoped Melody would think so too.

"Dean?"

"Oh, right. Sorry, Mia. My mind's wandering a lot lately."

"A sure sign that you're in love!" She grinned at him.

He hunched his shoulders. "Okay, gardenia because I was instructed to find a flower that reminded me of Melody, and this one does."

"Because…" Mia prompted.

"Because gardenias are beautiful and temperamental, but strong. They'll thrive if you give them everything they need to grow. And I have a feeling that's a lot like Melody. The leaves are really close to the color of her eyes, and the scent—" Dean paused and breathed deeply. "The scent is like Melody—unique and intoxicating."

"Perfect. And you got the fact sheet I gave you about them, right?"

"Right. And you're ready for the rest of my plan if everything goes the way I hope it will later today, right? It's kind of detailed. I have a lot of weeks planned out."

"Officer Dean," Mia patted his arm again, "I do surprises for a living. Trust me. I'll have the first delivery to *your* Melody within the hour. The rest is up to you. Now go!"

Dean went. He had about an hour, which was just enough time to get done the rest of what he needed to do. He'd learned that he needed to seduce Melody's mind before he tried to jump her bones. *Jump her bones* had been Nana's way of putting it. He'd tried to argue with the savvy old woman, but she'd skewered him with blue eyes that were so much like his that he could never hide anything from her.

"Did you not tell me she fled your *attentions* at the end of your date?"

He'd had to admit—again—that Nana was right. Everything had been going really well until one kiss had turned into another and another and she'd fled.

"Fine, Nana. I hear you. I'll seduce her mind. But what the hell does that actually mean?"

"Language, Dean Alessandro. Now, where was I? Oh, yes. Mental seduction. The concept is simple. The application of the concept, perhaps not so simple. Here is what you must strive to do—you must make her feel as if, in every room she enters, she is the best-loved woman there. If you can make her feel like that, your life together will be magnificent."

Bittersweet memories had darkened Nana's lined face.

"You miss him a lot, don't you?"

His Nana had smiled with such brilliance that beauty blazed through the years to make her look, for a moment, like a young girl in love again. "Yes, I miss your grandfather every day. But I have my memories of the fifty-two wonderful years we spent together. Your grandfather seduced my mind—and then I happily invited him to seduce the rest of me." Her eyes glittered mischievously.

"So, tell me how he did it. Uh, but not too graphically."

Nana giggled girlishly and sipped her limoncello, considering. "I think at the heart of it was the fact that my Alessandro made me feel as if he thought I was the most fascinating person he'd ever met. He was interested in *me*, not just my body parts. He showed me, day after day, year after year, that he cared about my thoughts, my desires, my dreams, and because I knew he cared about me like that, I knew our love would last."

Her nostalgia warmed him. "And it did last."

"You are very like your grandfather. I know you can do this—you can show Melody that your love is deep and strong enough to last."

So, Dean had set out to seduce Melody's mind.

He was going to send her flowers. Lots of flowers. But not make the "mistake most *idiota* men make when sending women flowers," as Nana had said, referring to the generic bouquets of red roses men purchase on autopilot when they're in trouble, just out of trouble, or worried about getting in future trouble. "To make it meaningful, choose a flower that represents Melody, and then find unusual ways to gift her with that flower. She'll know you put thought into it, and *that* will make her put more thought into you."

"Flowers done," Dean muttered aloud as he headed

into the little restaurant after double-checking to be sure the bookstore across the street was open. "And now for the rest of my plan…"

• • •

The deliveryman from Flush Floral gave Dean a small nod of recognition as he left the Siren Tours office. Dean brushed at a spot of invisible lint on his shirt, and then the tinkling bell announced his entrance to the shop. He thought it was a good sign that Melody didn't even look up from the package she held in her hands.

"Well, well, well, hello there, handsome," Harmony welcomed him with a clap.

"Hi, Harmony," Dean said. "Nice to see you again." He was speaking to the tall blonde, but his gaze was trapped on Melody.

At the sound of his voice, Melody's head snapped up. "Oh! Dean! It's you." She clutched the box against her chest, her cheeks turning an adorable pink.

"It's definitely me." He walked over to her, looking pointedly at the small bouquet she held in her hands. "I hope you like it."

"I do! It's beautiful and it smells delicious. But, um, what is it?"

"It's easier to show you than tell you." Dean held out his hand for the delicate bouquet. "May I?"

"Okay, sure." She handed him the cluster of three gardenias held together by a sea-green ribbon tied to a barrette. Then, just like Mia had showed him, Dean gently placed the flowers in Melody's hair over her left ear. "Oh!"

Melody exclaimed, touching the bouquet softly as she peered at her reflection in the large front window. "It's so pretty, and now the smell will follow me around all day."

"So, you like it?" Dean asked.

"Yes! Thank you, but you didn't need to send me anything," Melody said.

"I didn't need to, but I wanted to. And gardenias remind me of you."

"Really? Why that particular flower?" Harmony asked, joining them as they continued to check out Melody's reflection.

Dean recited the words he'd practiced with Mia, ending with, "So, these are for your eyes." He sent the florist and Nana a flood of silent thank-yous as both women's smiles widened.

"He is right," Harmony said. "The leaves are the same color as your eyes."

"Thanks again," Melody said. "It's a lovely gift." A customer entered the store, pulling Harmony's attention away from them, and Melody lowered her voice. "I'm really sorry about running out on you like that last night. I was afraid you wouldn't want to see me again. And I can explain. Sort of. If you give me the chance."

"You don't have anything to explain or apologize for—I owe you the apology. I went too fast. It was unchivalrous of me."

"No, really. It's my issue—my problem."

Dean tucked a stray strand of curling copper hair behind her left ear. "How about we talk about it over lunch? Can you take a break?"

"She can," Harmony said from across the room. "And

don't hurry back. I can handle things here." She looked at Melody and her voice lost some of its musical lightness. "And I want to be able to tell Rhapsody that everything worked out for you two."

Melody grabbed her purse and then hooked her arm through Dean's, pulling him to the door. "Sounds good. See you later." She waved absently at her cousin as they hurried outside.

Chapter Nine

"Sorry about Harmony. She is a little too interested in my—" Melody began, but Dean cut her off.

"Let's make a deal. You'll stop apologizing about your family, no matter how badly they embarrass you, *if* you don't hold me responsible for whatever embarrassing thing my family does or says when you meet them, and that includes stories about my short-lived, unfortunate baseball phase."

Her stomach flip-flopped. "When I meet your family?"

"Sadly for you, I think that's inevitable."

"I don't know, Dean." She considered, following his lead down the sidewalk. "That sounds pretty serious."

"Then we'll talk about it when we feel like being serious, but right now how about we focus on lunch?"

"Deal, but does that mean we can't talk about your unfortunate baseball phase?" she snickered.

"Let's leave the embarrassing details to my family, okay?"

"Hmm, well, okay, but I think I might enjoy embarrassing details—when they're not about me."

He took her hand and kissed the back of it lightly. She contained the cacophony of excited giggles pressing against her throat.

"I hope you're hungry," he said.

"I am. I didn't eat breakfast this morning." She couldn't. Not after everything that happened at home the night before. She let out a ragged sigh.

"I couldn't eat this morning either. All I could think about was seeing you again." Dean kept her arm wrapped through his and cut across several streets, heading the shortest way to Lombard Street.

"So, you really wanted to see me again even though I ran away from you last night," she finally said.

She didn't phrase it as a question, but Dean answered it anyway. "I really wanted to see you again." He guided her across Lombard Street, and headed up Fillmore. "If I hadn't been such an oaf, you wouldn't have had to run away."

"I didn't think you were an oaf. At least, I don't think I thought you were an oaf." She made a mental note to look up the word.

"What did you think?" he asked.

Between the haunting visions and voices and the way her chest fluttered when she was around him, she wasn't exactly sure how she felt about anything. She shrugged. "I thought you were a good kisser," she said, remembering the surge of excitement he'd unleashed when his lips locked on hers.

"Thank you, miss." Dean beamed as he guided her across the street to the welcoming entrance of Books, Inc.

Melody pursed her lips questioningly. "Is this a restaurant and a bookstore?"

"No, it's just a bookstore—my favorite bookstore in town, actually. Nana and I have been coming here since it opened. I thought you might like to pick out a book and take it to lunch with us."

"A book? Really? I love books!" Without waiting for him to open the door for her, Melody hurried inside.

Dean let out a deep sigh of relief and followed her.

"Hey there, Dino! Good to see you again," called the tall, studious man who was sitting on a stool behind the front register.

Dean waved. "Hi, Lester. How's business?"

"Good and bad, good and bad—like life in general." Lester cleared his throat, and Melody pulled her attention from the first table of books she'd stopped to browse through. "Well, hello there, gorgeous!" he said, tipping an invisible hat to Melody. His eyes flicked to Dean. "Boy, that's not your Nana."

"Nope, definitely not." Dean smiled proudly.

"Show some sense and introduce me. I may be old, but I'd have to be dead not to want to meet a beautiful woman."

Bashfulness heated Melody's cheeks as she fought to keep from slipping into one of the many aisles.

"Miss Melody Seirina, I would like to present you to the best bookseller I know, Mr. Lester Johnson." Dean stepped back and motioned for Melody to approach the desk.

Cautiously, she left the table of books and held out her hand, which the old man took, and with a smoothness that belied his advanced years, he bent over it with a neat and surprisingly courtly bow.

"It's nice to meet you, Mr. Johnson."

Lester's smile had the charm that came from a lifetime

of appreciating women. "It is entirely my pleasure, Miss Seirina. Please, call me Lester. Any friend of Dean's will need all the allies she can get."

Melody's stomach dropped until she caught a glimpse of his mischievous smirk.

"Lester! I didn't bring her in here so you could scare her away from me," Dean said with mock frustration.

"No, no, no, let me clarify. Melody, I meant you'll need allies to withstand Officer Kent's prodigious charms, and I can definitely help you with that."

Melody giggled.

"I'm not sure that's an improvement from your first statement," Dean muttered.

"I'm not helping?" Lester said.

Dean shook his head before turning to Melody. "Okay, now it's your choice. Pick any book in the store, and it's my gift to you."

"Nice gift, boy," Lester said. "You might be growing some sense under all that hair."

Melody snorted as she left Dean's side to move through the store, running her fingers reverently down the spines of hardback books, picking up one and then another before moving to another section.

Nothing in Tartarus was truly hers—everything was shared or borrowed, but not this. She would have her very own book. Her sisters would be so jealous. She stilled, her fingers lingering on a smooth cover. She couldn't tell the others about this gift or any romantic details. Harmony expected today to be the end of their relationship. The end of Dean.

Panic roared to life, making her fingers tremble. "It's

KRISTIN CAST & P.C. CAST

okay," she whispered, checking to make sure Dean hadn't
seen her trepidation. She didn't have to tell them. She *wouldn't*
tell them. She would let Harmony believe she'd done her
duty, and she would keep Dean to herself. She peered over at
him, seeing him chuckle as he flipped through the pages of a
children's book. It would be better this way. And she would
finally have something of her very own.

Taking a calming breath, she ran her hands through her
hair and focused on the world of unread stories. A slick,
cobalt cover caught her attention from across the store.

"Wow! Books about the ocean!" Melody shook off her
worries and made a beeline to the oceanography section.
Stretching her arm overhead, she lifted herself onto her
tiptoes to reach the shiny book.

"Hey, let me help you." With ease, Dean plucked the
hardback off the shelf.

Melody cooed and gasped over the glossy, full-color
pages filled with ocean life. "This is the one I want."

Dean glanced at the title. "*San Francisco Bay: Portrait of
an Estuary,*" he read aloud. "Will you be turned off if I tell
you I have no clue what an estuary is?"

She shrugged, not understanding how he could manage
to achieve such a thing. "Will I turn you off if I tell you that
I do know what it is?"

"Turned off? Hell, no! Brains are always a turn-on,
Miss Melody."

"Glad to hear it, Officer Dean." She nodded.

"Let's take it to Lester and make it yours." He snagged
her hand and whispered, "But what is an estuary?"

"It's where the mouth of a river meets the ocean—a
brackish tidal inlet, really."

86

Dramatically, Dean clutched his chest over his heart. "Be careful, I can only take so much of your sexy brainpower in public."

• • •

Melody was beaming at him, full wattage, as they left the store. With each look, Dean's heart did a funny little jumpy thing. Warm happiness took firm root within him and branched through his core.

"Okay, next stop is across the street," Dean said, pointing to the little restaurant called Seed & Salt. They entered, and he watched Melody's forehead furrow in concentration as she read through the vast chalkboard menu. "Will you trust me?" he asked her.

Her hands balled, then she relaxed a little and shrugged. "Okay, but I don't like to eat fish. Or shellfish. Or really anything that swims. And, um, I don't like blood. At all."

"I remember. Trust me. You won't find anything with blood here. It's a vegan restaurant."

"Vegan?"

"Yeah. You know, no meat of any kind. Also no dairy. Nothing in here comes from killing any living animal."

"Really?" Exuberance lifted her to the balls of her feet. "There are restaurants like that?"

It was strange how new the concept was to her, especially since it was right up her alley. But hell, he wouldn't have known either if he hadn't Yelped it the night before. She was new to the area, and probably new to the lifestyle too. He filed it away to ask about later.

"Really," said a tall waiter who approached Dean. "As

my girlfriend says, nothing we eat in this restaurant ever had a face." He handed Dean an old-fashioned picnic basket—the kind that was made of wicker and looked like something his Nana would have carried to picnics in Italy in her youth, mostly because the ancient picnic basket had, until last night, belonged to Nana. "Here ya go, Officer Dean. Enjoy."

"Thanks, Evan," Dean said. Then he crooked his arm for Melody again. "Shall we?"

She took his arm, saying, "Shall we what?"

"Shall we go on our picnic?"

Her nose wrinkled with excitement. "A picnic?"

"If you want," Dean said.

"Oh, I want! I want!"

Feeling better and better about Nana's advice, Dean walked arm-in-arm with Melody, cutting through the beautiful neighborhood that made up the Marina District. As they passed a wine bar, Dean ducked in, buying a chilled bottle of pinot grigio that was the color of moonlight. From there it was a quick walk to the Marina Green, where he spread out a red-and-white checked blanket.

"If you put out the food, I'll open the wine," Dean suggested.

Melody began to go through the basket, making happy noises as she discovered the cutlery, wineglasses, and neatly wrapped sandwiches.

Soon they were chewing enthusiastically as Melody propped her new book on the basket between them, and started thumbing through the glossy, full-color photographs, pausing to comment on the pictures of sea lions, dolphins, and otters.

Dean mostly listened to her talk about the sea life,

impressed by the depth of her knowledge. For every question he asked she had an answer, even though some of her answers seemed more in jest than in earnest—still, he was having a great time.

"How do you know so much about ocean life?" he asked, using his hand to shield his face from the sun.

"Classes, mostly. But also stories passed down from our elders. They're the ones with real experience." Her lips twitched with melancholy as she flipped through the pages.

"So, is your family full of marine biologists, or teachers, or—"

"Oh, Dean!" she interrupted, her excitement almost palpable. "You have humpbacks here! I've never talked with a humpback before. There are mostly just sperm whales in Greece. At least, that's what my mom used to tell me."

Intrigued by her sudden enthusiasm, he chuckled, "Do they talk, too?"

"Of course. All whales talk," she said matter-of-factly.

"Did your mom ever tell you what they would say?" Dean asked.

"Sperm whales sing songs to each other—males and females, entire families, talk and sing in clicks and squeaks. What do they say?" She grinned. "They talk about the same things we do when we talk to our families. Only they can say it at a depth of three thousand feet, and can stay underwater for ninety minutes."

"Does that book say all of that?"

"No," she laughed. "The whales say all of that. And my mom told me they're amazingly friendly. Young sperm whales like to have their heads rubbed. I love swimming," she mused. "And it would be amazing to swim with a whale."

"I guess it figures that as much as you love the water, you'd be a diver," Dean said.

"Oh, sure, I dive, but I've never gone down three thousand feet." She skimmed the last page before closing the book. "Or at least, not yet I haven't. The water at home doesn't get that deep."

"I hope you're kidding," Dean said as he refreshed her glass of wine.

Then, taking Dean by complete surprise, she leaned into him and kissed him softly on his cheek. "Thank you."

"For what?" he asked.

"For doing all of this." Melody made a gesture that took in their picnic lunch and the Marina. "It makes me feel special. So, thank you." She leaned into him again, and Dean sat very still as she gently kissed him on the mouth.

"That is the perfect thank you." Dean inhaled the sugary perfume floating from the gardenia nestled above her ear. "And you are special." He took her hand carefully in his.

"I'm glad you gave us another chance," Melody said, her lips brushing against his.

"You're worth it." The words came out shaky as his pulse thrummed under his skin, and he tensed against the urge to envelop her.

"Dude, I thought it was you!"

He bolted upright, almost knocking his head against Melody's. "Kait?" He squinted, his attitude sobering.

"And WTF with all of this?" She adjusted her bike and leaned over the handlebars. "A picnic?"

He could've throttled her for destroying whatever might have happened in the delicious moment he and Melody had just shared. "Melody Seirina, this is my oblivious partner,

Kait Lesnek. She likes to think of herself as my better half. Most of the time, I tend to agree with her."

"Wow, you must be special if Dean's already admitting my superiority in front of you." She leaned down, extending her hand to Melody.

"It's really nice to meet you. Dean's told me a lot about you," Melody said.

"Well, as of our next shift, Dean's going to be telling me a lot about you, too." Kait winked.

"Okay, well, sorry you have to take off and leave us to return to our really romantic picnic all alone here by ourselves," Dean said, shooing Kait away.

"No worries, Romeo. I'm going, I'm going. Oh, but first I'll give you my plus-one RSVP to your sis's wedding. Raquel said yes!"

Dean reached up to return the high five. "Congratulations! Raquel is one hot babe."

"Uh, I know, and I'm planning on making her *my* one hot babe. Hey, speaking of hot babes, you should bring Melody to your sis's wedding. It's going to be entertaining, if nothing else. Nice to meet you, Melody! I'm sure I'll be seeing you again soon!" Kait hopped on her bike and sped away.

"She seems nice," Melody said, twirling strands of her long hair.

"She is—nice and smart." He paused for a moment, his glance flicking between Melody and Kait's quickly vanishing figure. "Melody Seirina, would you please be my date one month from tomorrow at my sister's wedding? It's going to be a big dress-up affair, open bar, lots of dancing and family shenanigans."

His throat tightened as Melody chewed her lip, looking like he'd just asked her to visit a slaughterhouse with him.

"Hey, it's just a date," he said, angst softening his voice.

"It's your sister's wedding. That's important. And all of your family is going to be there. That's important, too."

"Well, sure. Yes. That's why I'm inviting you." He took both of her hands in his and caressed them gently. "Because *you're* important."

She pulled away, shoving her fists into her lap. "Can I give you an answer later?"

"Absolutely. Don't let it cause you any stress." Embarrassment warmed his cheeks and made him instantly regret asking.

Melody blew out a long breath and picked at the edge of her frayed jeans. "I want to explain about why I ran away last night." She stared out at the bay as she continued. "You weren't moving too fast. I liked your kisses. I liked them a lot. But then I started to feel, well, like I wanted *more* than that from you, and that scared me."

"Why?"

Still not looking at him, she blurted, "Because sex means bad things to me. Really bad things. Like, so bad that I'm not sure I'll ever be able to let myself have sex with you and now that you know, you probably won't want to keep seeing me and I completely understand because it's not normal and I wish it was different—I wish *I* was different—but I'm not."

Dean's heart squeezed. "Please look at me."

Melody reluctantly turned her gaze from the water to him. He saw her then—really saw her—afraid and vulnerable. Her chin trembled, and he stiffened with the realization that he'd made her feel that way.

That's why she ran.

Slowly, gently, he touched her cheek. "You're perfect just the way you are, and I'll make you a promise, right here, right now. I promise that I will never do anything again that makes you scared or uncomfortable. Melody, you always have the right to tell me to stop—no matter what. And I will."

"You want to keep seeing me?"

Dean wanted to tell her that he wanted to see *only* her, forever, but he knew he had to move slowly, carefully. So, he simply said, "Yes, Melody, I do. Would you go to dinner with me tomorrow night?"

"There's nothing I'd like more."

"Not even talking to whales?" he teased.

"Is it really that bad to come second to a whale?" She grinned and kissed him quickly, softly, on his cheek.

Dean thought his heart might explode. "When you put it like that, nope, it's not bad at all."

CHAPTER TEN

It'd been almost a month since he'd started dating Melody, and Dean hadn't been by Siren Tours since he'd met up with her for their picnic. Melody had alluded to some intense family drama, and instructed him not to speak to Harmony or even come near the store, so he hadn't. Not because he didn't want to—he was itching to find out what Harmony's issue was with him and his relationship with her cousin—but because he wouldn't betray her trust—something Melody didn't seem to give out freely.

But now he had an excuse.

He pulled out one of the flyers his sergeant had passed out at the beginning of his shift and marched toward Siren Tours.

"Melody can't get mad at me for doing my job." He swallowed hard. "At least, I hope not."

He entered the shop, relieved when he saw that it was free of customers. "Harmony!" he boomed a little too enthusiastically as he headed for the tall blonde. "You're just the Siren I wanted to see."

"Dean?" Shock shook her voice. "I didn't think I'd see you here again. And in your uniform. Melody didn't mention you worked for the police."

"Yes, ma'am." He tapped the shield fastened above his left breast pocket. "I'm one of the good guys."

"I can see that." She left her paperwork and circled the cashier's counter. "So, what brought you in this evening?"

"There was an attack not too far from here about one month ago. We still haven't caught the perpetrator. We don't want you to be alarmed, just aware." He handed her the flyer containing the SFPD tip line number, a few notes about the suspect, and a bulleted list of ways to stay safe in the city.

"An attack by someone in a costume? That sounds horrible." She read the rest of the page before setting it on the countertop. "Was anyone injured?"

"I'm afraid the victim lost his life." He shook away visions of the bloody scene and masked assailant. "But I'm not here just to give you that."

"Oh?" She set the paper on the countertop and crossed her arms over her chest.

"Do you have a problem with me?" He rushed through the sentence, making it sound curter than he'd planned. "Wait, don't answer that. Let me start again." He sighed. "I want to let you know that you don't have to worry about Melody."

"Worry about her?" Harmony smirked, the lines around her mouth deeper than he remembered. "She's a strong girl. I know she's able to take care of herself."

"Yes, she's very strong, and smart, and talented, and funny. I wouldn't do anything to risk losing her."

"Ah, I see," she said, slowly closing the gap between them.

"I know there's family stuff going on. She even told me not to come here, but I knew if I could just talk to you and show you that I'm a good guy, we could figure this out. Harmony, I won't hurt her."

"Oh, I know *you* won't hurt *her*."

Dean's stomach clenched instinctively. "What do you mean by that?"

"Hmm?" Harmony brushed past him, switching the front sign from OPEN to CLOSED.

"What are you not telling me?" His breath quickened as he moved his hand to hover above his baton.

"*Dean.*"

Harmony's voice was buttery and warm, and his ears throbbed with the beat of imagined music as he waited for her to say something more, *anything* more.

"*You don't need your weapons.*"

The world around him melted, and he knew nothing but her. "I don't need my weapons." His hand relaxed next to his side, and he let the illusory tune take hold.

"*Good. Now, let's go into my office.*"

• • •

It was only a little past eight, but the neon light hanging above the door to Siren Tours read CLOSED in glowing red letters.

"Huh," Melody mused as she pulled open the door. "Harm, you closing early? I came to grab my phone. I think I left it here." The only answer was the hum of fluorescent lights. "Harmony? Hello?"

"Melody!" The word was muffled, obstructed by the closed office door.

"Dean?" She ran to Harmony's office and jiggled the handle. Locked. "Dean? Are you in there?"

"Quiet!" Harmony seethed.

"Harmony?" Melody pressed her ear against the door. "What are you doing? Open the door!" Her fists thundered against the wood.

Don't let them take him.

"I won't!" Melody screamed against the ever-present voice whispering between her ears.

Her hands heated as scales surged to life from her fingers to her elbows. She tried the knob again. It caved under her grip, and she ferociously ripped it through the wood, splinters spraying from the new hole. She tore open the door. Her body sizzled against the change creeping up her arms and legs, threatening to engulf her.

"Melody, run!" Dean shouted as Harmony hurled herself against him. His body bounced off of hers, smacking into the brick wall behind him. Groaning, Dean crumpled to the floor.

Melody rushed to his side.

"She's the monster. The one that killed that man. Get out of here," he croaked. "Go." He blinked sluggishly before closing his eyes, his head lolling back against the brick.

"Melody, I—" Harmony began, but Melody's anger punched through her words.

"What's wrong with you?" she shrieked, rising to her feet. "Why would you do this?"

"I'm cleaning up your mess." Harmony's silvered scales

rippled as she spoke. "He's in danger, Melody. *You* put him there. How do you not see that?"

"*I* put him in danger? You would have killed him." She stepped toward Harmony, so close the waves of heat twisting off of her gray scales bit at her eyes. "And for what? Some ancient code? This isn't Greece, and we aren't the ruling species. We don't have the right to take this realm or murder innocent people. Our time here is over. We belong in Tartarus."

"You don't know what you're talking about." Harmony's temples pulsed.

"I know enough."

"Step back." Harmony's breath blew back strands of Melody's wild mane. "Sit down. It doesn't have to be this way."

"So you're going to change the rules, and let me have this one good thing in my life?"

Harmony sighed. "Melody, if you'd let me explain—"

"I'm tired of your lessons." She bent down and placed Dean's arm around her shoulders, hugging him against her side and hefting him to his feet.

"Melody?" He groaned and looked groggily around the room.

"It's fine. Everything's going to be fine," she assured him, turning her attention back to Harmony. "My mother trusted you to protect me, to make sure I was happy. *He* makes me happy. Don't you want that for me? Or do you just want to use me to break the stupid curse like you use the others?"

Harmony paused for three beats of Melody's hammering heart.

"Be sure about this, Melody. I don't know that I can shield you from whatever consequence this might carry."

Melody lifted her chin. "I'll take my chances."

Harmony took a deep breath. *"Dean, can you hear me?"*

He nodded listlessly.

"You don't remember coming here. You only remember meeting Melody outside the store. You decided to go out. You had a great time, but you drank too much and fell." Sadness crept into Harmony's voice as her scales faded, replaced by pink flesh. "I have to tell Rhapsody."

Melody swallowed against the hard lump building in her throat. "You know the best part about the humans? They're willing to stand up for what they believe is right." She adjusted Dean's arm around her shoulders and supported him as they hobbled out of the store.

CHAPTER ELEVEN

Melody twitched under the covers. Her heartbeat quickened and sweat beaded her body as the all-too-real dream unfolded.

"Jay, I got it! I got the job!" She snatched the freshly printed pages off the printer, and hugged the warm papers against her chest. "You are now talking to the newest member of St. David's Labor and Delivery Unit!"

There was a slight lag before he spoke, his voice tinny through the crackling reception. "I knew you would! Never doubted you for a minute."

"You're the best." Still uncomfortable in the bursts of silence between exchanges, she straightened and restraightened the job offer before plopping it on the side of the bed that remained neatly tucked in.

"We'll celebrate when I get home. Maybe finally take that trip to Hawaii we've been talking about."

"We deserve it. There's a lot to celebrate: my new job, your

freedom from the military, our wedding, when I'll no longer be Melanie Blackwell...our new normal life."

"A normal life. I like the way that sounds." His smile was audible. "I gotta get going. Should be able to make another call on Friday. I love you, Mel."

"I love you too, Jay. Be safe. I miss you." The line went dead.

After the abrupt ending of each phone call, she never felt like she'd said enough. What if she never spoke to him again? Did he know how much she loved him?

She fell back against her pillow and stretched her arm over the empty space next to her. "I miss you so much, Jay."

The doorbell rang, forcing Melody from the distant memory.

"Jay." She groggily stretched out her arm and ran her hand along the cool sheets of the undisturbed side of the bed.

The doorbell trilled again.

Melody's eyelids flew open and she sucked in her first conscious breath. "Coming!"

Please don't be Harmony. Or worse... She shuddered at the memory of Harmony's promise to contact Rhapsody after she'd made the decision to rescue Dean. *But that was a week ago.*

She plastered on a fake grin and opened the door.

"Ms. Seirina?" The bellman craned his neck to see around the large potted plant he gripped with both hands.

"Yes." Melody caught a glimpse of her Medusa-like shadow, and self-consciously smoothed down her hair.

"I guess I should clarify. Are you Ms. *Melody* Seirina? There are quite a few of you staying with us. It can get a little confusing." He chuckled nervously.

"You have the right Seirina." She smiled.

A bead of sweat rolled down his temple as he shifted his weight.

"Oh, I'm sorry. That must be heavy. Come in." She padded out of the way and held open the door.

He waddled inside and let out a small grunt as he squatted to place the planter on the floor. "There's a great florist not far from here. I can run out and grab some plant food if you'd like."

Melody shrugged. "I haven't cared for a plant before, but it makes sense that it would need to eat."

"I'll have the finest plant cuisine to you in no time." He brushed off his hands and straightened his uniform. "Oh, it also arrived with this." He reached into his vest pocket and handed her a small white rectangle. "Have a great day, Ms. Seirina."

She waited until the door was firmly closed behind him to open the miniature envelope. "This past month has been pure magic. I hope it never ends," she read aloud, instantly knowing who the boxy handwriting belonged to. "Dean!" she gushed, shoving her nose against the flower's familiar velvety buds. The gardenia's saccharine scent enveloped her, and she understood, for the first time, what it meant to have butterflies in her stomach.

Silently, she'd applauded herself for keeping Dean in the dark about his near-fatal run-in with Harmony. Not that he remembered—Harmony had made sure of that—but there were times when his cop instinct began to guide him down that treacherous path.

He's in danger, Melody. You put him there.

"Well, now he is. Since you tried to kill him," she huffed.

At least she hadn't had to worry about her sisters finding out anything. They were all too busy doing stuff Melody tried hard not to think about or overhear. There had been some tricky moments, but she'd pulled it off.

Pushing aside her trepidation and focusing on the happiness Dean brought, she twirled around the living room. Nearly tripping over her gift, she let out a breathy laugh and steadied herself against an accent table.

Her gaze lingered on the vibrant leaves before lifting to meet her reflection's. Her cheeks were bubblegum pink with mirth, and she pressed her cool fingers against them. She'd answered the door without putting on any makeup, but that didn't matter. The skin around her eyes and lips remained smooth, and her forehead wrinkled only when she lifted her eyebrows. She stared at herself intently, raising each eyebrow one at a time, and feeling extraordinarily human when unlined skin rested across her still brow.

She dropped her hands, releasing the card onto the table. The back of the card stared up at her, and on it the words *To: Mel.*

"Mel?" She cringed.

A nauseating palpitation took hold inside her chest, squeezing her lungs and forcing her breath out in labored grunts.

I love you, Mel. The shadow of a dream stirred and her vision doubled. Over the past month she'd gotten better at holding the flickering visions at bay, but she needed answers and today she had more than images. She had a name.

She darted from the living room and raced to her bedside table. She grabbed her phone and pressed the blue

Internet icon, thankful she'd listened to all of the technology tutorials Harmony had bored them with.

"Okay, Google, if you can bring me information about anything in this realm, show me Melanie Blackwell." She jabbed the search square and waited the 0.14 seconds for Google to return with an answer. "Wow." She rolled the phone over, expecting to see residue from some sort of other-realmly magic. "You're fast."

There were pages and pages of results. Too many if Melody wanted to continue living her own life. "Hmm." She squinted, forcing herself to remember more of the dream. "Melanie Blackwell, St. David's. And search." The second search result made her feel like her heart was lodged in her throat.

Melanie Lane Blackwell Obituary—Visitation and Funeral Information—Floral Haven.

With a shaky finger, she tapped the blue lettering. The obituary was short, mentioning the family members she was survived by, the career at St. David's she'd worked the entirety of her short life to excel at, and the fiancé she'd loved dearly. Melody scrolled down to the page's "Memories" section and read boxes and boxes of well wishes and comments left by friends and family. Hillary Kerns had posted a picture with the caption, *Such a happy day!*

Melody couldn't move. She could barely breathe as she studied the women in the picture. One was Melanie. She recognized her from her photo accompanying the obituary. Her deep brown doe eyes glistened off the screen as she smiled at the camera, showing off her left hand and the sparkling diamond ring perched on her finger. The same ring Melody had seen in her vision, flickering and ghostlike, on her first day working at Siren Tours. But what made the pit in her stomach deepen, threatening to swallow her whole, was the woman Melanie clutched next to her.

She swiped her fingers over the image, zooming in on the woman's smiling face. "I know her."

Three swift knocks echoed from the door. Melody flinched so hard she lost her grip on the phone. It slapped against the floor. The knocks repeated, this time with more force. Melody plucked her phone up off of the carpet, slipped it into her pocket, and tightened the robe around her before scurrying down the hall.

"That was *quick*." The last word came out a strained whisper.

"I won't bother to ask who you were expecting." Melody's stomach knotted as Rhapsody's predatory glare traced her body.

"Don't be rude, Melody," Harmony scolded.

"Oh, right. Sorry." She cleared her throat and offered a sweeping gesture toward the living room. "Please, come in."

Rhapsody brushed past her, sliding off her trench coat and tossing it across Melody's shoulder. Sand-crusted droplets seeped through Melody's bathrobe, spreading sticky salt against her skin.

"Rhapsody just arrived," Harmony explained.

"And you are the first one of my girls I wanted to see." Beads of water dripped from Rhapsody's hair and splatted around her feet.

Melody lifted her gaze from the floor, taking in the gentle slopes of Rhapsody's body. "Me? Why me?" she asked, even though she already knew.

Rhapsody wore her true skin as she would a tailored suit.

Streaks of sunlight glinted off her honey-colored scales, and they rippled shades of deep gold the dim light in Tartarus could never reveal.

Harmony sighed. "We're aging quickly. We don't have much time left, and you're not doing what has to be done."

"Yes I am." Her meek tone revealed the lie.

Rhapsody scoffed. "Harmony tells me you've been with the same man for weeks now, yet he's still alive. You mustn't play with your food, my dear."

"But I'm not. I—"

"Stop lying!" Rhapsody barked with unabashed ferocity, her carnivorous gaze fastened to Melody. "At least you seem to be good at one thing. Your makeup looks…" She took a step closer, squinting.

Oh no. Melody's stomach clenched. *Please don't notice I'm not wearing any. Please.* She flinched as each of Rhapsody's inspective looks struck her clean skin.

"Wonderful. Completely flawless."

The tension in Melody's chest unraveled, and she took a full breath for the first time since opening the door.

"I'm impressed." Rhapsody pursed her lips as if the compliment left a bitter trail across her tongue. "That should only make it easier for you to find a suitable sperm donor." She tossed back her wet hair, catching her reflection in the mirror. Sauntering to the glass, she said, "Oh, I wish this beauty would last. How we would rule this realm as we did so many centuries ago—our species free again." She cleared her throat. "And, Melody, I want proof you're completing your true task. Bring me a finger, or a toe." Slick white teeth cut through her smile. "Maybe even the human's head. And I want it today."

"Today? But I can't today. I have to—"

"You have to do only what I say you must do. You have no other purpose here. Your life is simple, really."

Again, Melody averted her eyes to the floor.

"Just do what you came here to do." Desperation rested in Harmony's voice.

"Okay," Melody whispered.

Harmony's shadow floated closer, until it mixed with her own. "I wouldn't tell you to do something you weren't capable of. It's in your nature. It's part of who you are." She lowered her voice, and Melody had to strain to hear her. "This will bring you more joy than you think you have now. You'll see."

Laughter like barking seals invaded the room. "*To Mel. This past month has been pure magic. I hope it never ends. Human men are such imbeciles.*" Rhapsody continued to chortle as she pinched the note between her fingers and tore it down the middle.

"Wait, you can't…" Melody's words faded as bits of paper drifted to the floor.

"You like him?" Rhapsody's damp black bangs cut across her forehead, shielding her bushy eyebrows with every questioning glance.

Melody nodded.

Rhapsody rested her hands on her hips. "He doesn't want you. Not the *real* you. He's only interested in the pieces he can invade."

Melody remained silent as Rhapsody repeated lines from the same speech she'd given countless times. But Dean wanted her. And not in the way guys wanted girls in the thoughtless college movies she'd watched with her sisters. She knew he wanted her in a sweet, slow-motion, all-consuming, Nicholas-Sparks-movie sort of way. At least, she was pretty sure that was how he wanted her.

"And you're naïve if you think anything different." Rhapsody's famous final line snapped Melody back to attention.

"I know it might be hard to hear after how nice he's been, but it's true," Harmony said.

"So, today you will go out on the tour boat, find a human, and make him yours. Do it, or I'll make your boy toy mine." Rhapsody snatched up her coat and threw open the door. "Have fun."

Harmony offered an apologetic smile as she followed Rhapsody into the hall.

Melody bent down, collected the torn bits of Dean's note, and placed them in her pocket. Defeated, she walked on autopilot to her bedroom closet. "Okay. I can do this." She breathed and began pawing through her uniforms for the tiny outfit she had to wear while on boat duty. "It's just one person. One life. A life for the possibility of a new life. It's not that big of a deal." Her throat tightened with the lie. She sighed, held the sailor outfit in front of her, and turned to the full-length mirror resting in the corner. She still looked like herself, but she'd changed during the journey between realms. So much so that she wondered if the part of her capable of taking life still existed. Through the tension in her jaw, she forced a wide, fake, Siren Tours smile.

CHAPTER TWELVE

"This isn't me. It's not right. I can't do it." Melody sank down behind the main bar of the packed cruise ship.

"Can't do what?" Aria asked, unloading a sleeve of plastic cups and stacking them behind the bar.

"This." Melody gestured toward the mass of tourists. "Choose a man, and, *you know*."

Aria nodded. "Oh, yeah. I know exactly how you're feeling."

"You do?"

"Definitely. My first trip up here, I was scared to death. I mean, completely terrified."

"You were? Oh, Aria, that makes me feel so much better. I was starting to think there was something really wrong with me."

"No, not at all." She waved dismissively. "We all feel that way. I mean, human men seem so macho, so intimidating. But once you realize they're just sacks of dough begging to be shaped into whatever you want, they completely lose all their power."

Confusion pinched Melody's brow. "That's not really what's bothering me."

Aria continued, unfazed. "I'm already on my fourth trip up. Haven't gotten pregnant yet." She sank down next to Melody and whispered, "Just between us, I hope I never do. The sun. The men. The delicious way their bones crunch between your teeth." She closed her eyes and took a deep breath, shivering slightly. "I'd miss it."

Melody didn't hide her disgust. "That's disturbing."

"You're funnier than I thought you'd be." Aria laughed and batted Melody's arm before standing. "You seem really nice, which can make this whole thing that much harder. And I'm guessing it didn't work out with that guy you brought on board a few weeks ago?" She didn't wait for an answer. "Too bad. He was cute. And fit. The muscular ones always taste better. Anyway," she paused and popped an almond in her mouth, "how about I help you out?"

Melody stood. "You'd do that?"

"Of course. Us Sirens have to stick together if we're ever going to get out of Tartarus and make this our home." She placed a knife and two limes on a cutting board, and slid it to the open counter space in front of Melody. "Cut these. I'll help you look, and even make contact, but staring out at them like a hungry tiger isn't cool."

Melody did as she was told, although looking around the room while using a knife was a bit complicated and dangerous.

"There, in the blue hat." Aria leaned over. "You see him?"

Melody scanned the room until her eyes settled on the

man. He was short and stocky, with the swollen chest of a bullfrog. "Yeah. Now what?"

"We get his attention. Laugh and hop up and down like you're really excited. The jumping really gets 'em." She stuck out her chest. "And as he looks over, make eye contact and smile."

Melody smiled in preparation.

"But more of a sexy smile. Not one you'd give if someone was about to take your picture."

Melody tried again.

"Don't worry. We'll work on it."

Melody caught Blue Hat's eye and smiled coyly, but instantly dropped the cute girl act the second she saw the little boy clutching his fingertips. "He's a dad," she muttered to Aria.

"So? They're all someone's dad or brother or son or whatever." She rolled her eyes before pointing out another potential victim. "How about Green Mohawk? I bet that'd be a wild ride."

Melody looked up in time to see Green Mohawk gently kiss the cheek of a thin young woman with long purple hair. "Looks like that's his girlfriend."

Aria put her hands on her hips and cocked her head to the side. "Do you want my help or not?"

"Yes, of course I do." Melody let out a defeated sigh. "Rhapsody came to my room this morning. She's mad that this is taking me so long," she said, purposefully leaving out the rest of the convoluted tale.

"Whoa. Rhapsody's here?" Aria chewed her bottom lip. "You have to get this done, Melody."

Melody poked at the lime slices with the tip of the knife. "I know."

"I don't think you do." Aria looked around the room, fear igniting her dark eyes. "Rhapsody will make sure you're left here. She's done it before over a lot less."

"Left here? She can't do that. It's not like you need a key to pass through the portal."

"But do you know how to find it?" Aria asked.

Melody searched her thoughts. She remembered Tartarus, hot pain searing her lungs, that voice, then the surface, the sun. And Dean. She shook her head.

"Exactly. You need a Caretaker, a Siren like Harmony, to find it. Left here without one, you'll age, dry up, and die in a matter of weeks. But I've also heard other things." She lowered her voice to a barely audible whisper. "Rhapsody has killed some of our sisters herself. She's dangerous."

Laughter roared from a group of celebrating tourists. "We shouldn't be talking about this." She collected a few empty cups and cleared her throat. "Now, the next guy I choose will be the one. That's why they say third one's the charm."

Aria went back to searching the room, but Melody felt caged by the new information. Rhapsody had already threatened Dean. Would she kill them both if Melody didn't do as she'd instructed her?

"There we go. And he has red hair, too. You would have the cutest ginger baby." Aria cheered. "Check him out. He's at your two o'clock."

Melody glanced at the digital clock hanging above the tour information booth.

"Not literally two o'clock," Aria grunted. "Over there."

She pointed to the port-side exit. Leaning against the doorway was the redhead. He fidgeted with his wedding band, twisting it each time his head tilted back with shoulder-shaking laughter.

"But he's married."

Aria shrugged. "That doesn't matter. And I have a feeling about this one. Now, laugh."

She jabbed her fingers into Melody's side.

"Ouch!" She yipped and rubbed at her ribs. "What was that for?"

Aria grimaced. "I was tickling you. But it got his attention. Give him a sultry smile and a little wave."

Her gaze found his, and she offered a sexy smile. Well, her lips curled somewhere between a sneer and a grin, but whatever it was, it worked. He patted his friend on the back, and sauntered to the bar.

"Aria! He's coming over here. What do I do? What do I do?" She turned to face Aria, her hand clutching the knife.

"First, put this down." Aria peeled back her fingers and removed the knife. "Waving that thing around makes you look like a killer." She snorted. "Ironic, isn't it?"

Melody frowned.

"Anyway, just be yourself. You're gorgeous. Plus, a lot of men want a wide-eyed, confused woman," she said, fluffing the ends of Melody's copper hair.

"What?"

"Exactly. And tell him there's a party downtown at that Walgreens warehouse on Bay Street, and you'll meet him there around ten. It's completely abandoned, so some of the girls and I use it for our hookups. No cameras, no cops, lots of privacy. And he'll do whatever you ask, so you can

make him be as gentle or as rough as you like. Have fun."
She winked and grabbed a tray of fresh drinks before flitting
away and into the crowd.

Have fun? They kept tossing that out there like having
sex with, then killing someone was a party.

"Hi."

He was here. It really had begun, and she couldn't run
away or change her mind. It had to be him, and it had to be
tonight. *This is for Dean. It's all to protect Dean.*

"Hi." She smiled, and this time just the thought of Dean
made it a genuine Melody smile, not a "sexy," twisted mess
of a thing.

"You have a beautiful smile."

When Dean told her she was beautiful her cheeks
flamed and her heart skipped. Hearing the compliment now
only made her queasy. "Thank you."

"I couldn't help but notice it from all the way over
there." He pointed across his chest. The thin gold band
had vanished from his finger, leaving a pale, hairy outline in
its place. "I also couldn't help but notice the way you were
looking at me."

Melody squinted at his finger, "Wait, aren't you…" She
let the words trail off. It didn't matter. Nothing about him
mattered if she wanted to stay alive and protect Dean.

"Aren't I what?" He licked his lips as he spoke to the
Siren Tours logo stretched across her chest.

For a moment, Dean slipped from her mind along with
the empathy she held for the human race. This guy was a
creep. The exact kind of man Rhapsody spent so much of
her time preaching about. Melody wouldn't sleep with him.
She'd save that for someone who deserved her. But no one

had to know that part. Aria had ravaged countless men, and still wasn't pregnant.

She'd end him like Rhapsody wanted, but she wouldn't give herself to him. She'd *never* give herself to anyone like him.

Melody cleared her throat in an attempt to draw his attention to her eyes and away from her breasts. Her face wrinkled in disgust, although it didn't matter—he still hadn't looked up.

"Aren't you tired of doing all of this touristy stuff?" she continued.

"You have something else in mind, sweetheart?"

"There's a party on Bay Street. At the Walgreens warehouse. I can meet you there around ten," she recited.

Finally, eye contact. She readied herself to have to attempt to command him, but she hadn't tried to use her Siren powers since meeting Dean, so her chances of success were pretty slim.

"I had other plans tonight, but I can get out of them and meet you instead." His gaze rolled up and down her torso. "You going to wear that?"

Melody rolled her shoulders forward, trying to make her chest appear smaller. "I'm not sure."

"You should. It fits you perfectly. Really brings out the color of your eyes."

She looked down at the white-and-blue uniform. "My eyes are green."

"And beautiful."

Melody felt sick and small and powerless. She opened her mouth to call off the rendezvous, but was cut off by the PA system. Aria's smooth voice calmly instructed passengers on how to disembark as soon as the boat was finished docking.

"Hate to cut this short, but it sounds like I need to get in line. I'll see you tonight." He fired two finger guns at her and quickly returned to his comrades.

Melody waited until he had stepped off the boat to drop her head into her hands.

"So, you meeting him?" Aria emptied a tray of trash into the garbage can.

"He thinks I am, but I really don't want to."

"If you don't go tonight, I'll have to tell Rhapsody. I don't want her finding out from someone else and thinking I had anything to do with the mistakes you're making. We're going back to Tartarus in a couple weeks, and I won't be left behind. Get it together, Melody. The hard part is over. You should be excited." Aria snatched a damp bar towel and stomped away.

"I *should* be excited, but I'm not like you," Melody muttered as tears burned her eyes.

CHAPTER THIRTEEN

"Hello? Siren girl, you here?" The redhead's words bounced around the empty warehouse. "Shit, there's no way I'm being stood up by some wannabe sailor bitch."

"I'm here." Melody stepped out from the shadows. Dust floated listlessly in the shards of moonlight cutting through the black around her. She tugged at her uniform's short skirt.

"Knew you'd come." He laughed, a dry, hacking sound that grated against her ears. "So, where's the party?"

"They must have changed locations. Funny how things like that happen." Having no confidence in her ability to lie and flirt convincingly, Melody felt miniscule and stupid when she spoke.

He stepped closer, too close. His fingers traced up her arms like hungry spiders. "If you wanted to be alone with me, all you had to do was say the magic word." He licked his lips, and they glistened in the silver light. "You do know the magic word, don't you?" He filled the space in front of her. Every word blew back strands of her hair.

She shook her head, the motion so slight he might not have even noticed.

"Let me teach you." He leaned in, the heat from his moist lips threatening to meet hers.

Every nerve in her body was alive and on fire. "Stop!" She pushed against his chest with foreign strength.

His ass smacked into the ground, tossing up a white sheet of debris. "What the fuck?!" He scampered backward. Glass crushed beneath his hands and he let out a sharp yelp. He held his fist against his chest and scurried to his feet.

She looked down at her arms. Sheets of emerald twinkled in the moonlight. "No," she gasped, bringing her hands to her face. Newborn scales bristled under her touch. Her heart thundered with such ferocity, her fishlike skin shook.

"Wait!" She lunged forward, trying to catch him.

"Stay the fuck away from me!"

He hit her. Hard.

The slap knocked her to her knees and sent light swirling through her vision. Melody's cheek ached and stung. He'd sliced her with something. The shard of glass protruding from his palm. Blood slid away from her wound, peppery and hot.

The redhead raced away, retracing his path through the empty warehouse.

"Stop!" she cried, and scrambled to get her feet under her. The room spun as she stood, and she held out her arms to keep from falling.

He was near the exit, a thin sheet of plastic the only shield from the streets of San Francisco and the rest of the Mortal Realm.

"Stop!" she wailed again.

Gold appeared from the darkened corner of the building and flashed in front of the makeshift door.

There was a wet scream and the sound of liquid raining down on the floor. Then silence.

The shimmering specter lumbered forward, the man's writhing body carving a blood-soaked streak in the dusty floor behind her.

Melody sucked in air. "*Rhapsody.*"

Rhapsody had made the shift to her true predatory self. Her jaw expanded, hanging low and heavy, too big to belong to her golden frame. Thin, needlelike fangs jutted out from her puckered, scaly mouth, while blood-soaked whiskers hung limply, vibrating with her breath. Her vocal cords constricted by her True Form, she emitted a series of clicks and high-pitched shrieks before shaking the man's body from the long, daggerlike claws she used as skewers.

Red gushed from the bite in the man's neck. It pooled around his head and shoulders as his body shuddered and he gasped impotently for air.

Melody dropped to the floor and frantically covered his neck with her hands. She had to stop the bleeding. Blood as warm as Ghirardelli's hot chocolate pulsed against her palms. He tried to speak, but only burbled scarlet froth. His frightened, pleading eyes stared up at her.

"I'm sorry," she whispered, unsure whether blood or tears were warming her cheeks.

Soon, too soon, the waves of blood stopped crashing against her hands, and his expression went slack. Glassy doll eyes stared up at her as the last bits of life seeped from his body.

"What are you?" Rhapsody was on her, jerking her head

back by a fistful of her hair. Rhapsody's face was human again, but just as frightening. Blood dripped off of her teeth to join the rivulets sliding down her chin.

"I'm different! I tried to tell you before!"

Melody's neck was exposed, and Rhapsody's ferocious gaze seemed trapped on her pulsing jugular.

"Please don't kill me," she begged.

Rhapsody opened her mouth and dragged a bloody claw across her tongue. It left a glossy crimson streak on her taste buds. "Be still."

Melody was rigid, each inhale shallower than the last in fear of making any unwanted movements. A damp finger swiped her uninjured cheek, rubbing harder and harder until her flesh was raw and bruised.

"Well, well, well, that is a pleasant surprise." Rhapsody released her fist from Melody's hair and beamed a nightmarish smile. "You have no makeup on."

"No, I don't," Melody said softly.

"You've been here a month. You should look at least a decade older than you do."

"I know," Melody said miserably.

"Why didn't you tell anyone about this, you foolish girl?"

"I—I…" Melody scrambled for an explanation that wouldn't further infuriate the enraged Siren, but fear muddied her thoughts.

"You know, you're exactly what we have waited centuries for." Rhapsody leaned in closer, blood hanging metallic on her breath. "You're the beginning of our salvation."

CHAPTER FOURTEEN

Melody's stomach churned. "No." She shook her head. "I'm no one's salvation."

Rhapsody's laughter lacked real humor. "Do tell, then, *why* aren't you aging like the rest of us?"

"Something happened to me on the way to this realm, and since then I've been having memories of a different life. A *human* life," she blurted.

With inhuman strength, Rhapsody lifted Melody to her feet and pulled her to stand before a dirty window where their reflections stared back at them.

"Change into your True Form with me. Now!" With a flick of her head, Rhapsody's human face shifted to reveal the Siren again. When Melody hesitated, she hissed a warning. Her breath sent waves of nausea coursing through Melody.

The young Siren stared into the mirrored glass, drew a deep breath, and opened herself to the fear and anger Rhapsody uncovered within her. She clung tightly to those vulnerable and violent emotions, and by doing so found her True Form.

Her skin shivered and Melody's reflection quivered and changed, but she didn't look like the creature lurking beside her. In her True Form, Melody's body was the same emerald as her eyes, just as Rhapsody's True Form reflected the honey gold of her irises. And like Rhapsody, Melody's face took on an aquatic look. Her eyes had doubled in size, and her teeth were sharper. Her hair had changed to long, undulating coils of copper that moved as if they were submerged in an invisible ocean. Her neck had lengthened, and grown small gill slits, but it hadn't thickened like Rhapsody's. And except for the emerald scales that covered all of her skin, and the delicate webbing between her fingers and toes, her body hadn't changed at all.

"Sssssssssssshift!" Rhapsody screeched and gnashed her teeth together.

"I did! This is as far as I change! Rhapsody, this *is* my True Form." Melody choked back sobs. "I told you something happened to me. I'm no one's savior—I'm *broken.*"

With another flick of her head, Rhapsody's face shifted back to its human form. She stared at Melody in disgust.

"Return to your human form. Like this you're too hideous for me to look at," she commanded.

Melody did as she was told, trying to edge away from Rhapsody, but the Siren followed her, still staring at her ageless skin.

"It's incredible, really," Rhapsody said. "I didn't expect the change in your True Form, though I suppose it shouldn't surprise me. Your blood has been diluted for generations. It had to be to break Hera's wretched curse." She shuddered delicately. "It is unfortunate how much of your humanity you retain when you shift. It's pathetic, really, but as we know all too well, with each gift comes a price."

"I—I just don't know if this—" Melody made a gesture that circled her lineless face "—has anything to do with my blood being diluted, or breaking the curse. Something human took over my body, *keeps* taking over. I know her name. I did research. She drowned the same day we arrived." Melody paused, the realization of her words momentarily overpowering her. "I think—I think that's why this is happening."

"How about you leave the thinking to me." Rhapsody sauntered to the dead man, reached down, and dipped a finger in the scarlet pool. Licking it contemplatively, she studied Melody. "That's why you were able to take that human lover. You don't have to shift when you mate with him." She spat red foam. "You truly are special."

"But we haven't had sex. He's waiting until I'm ready."

"Does he know what you really are?"

"No, but he will."

Rhapsody scoffed. "You tell him, and he'll leave you. Or worse, if you show him he'll either go mad or hunt you down and kill you like an animal."

"You mean like you would?"

Rhapsody's expression softened. She inhaled deeply and swayed slightly as her scales melted into her skin. "I would never hurt you." Her bare, blood-streaked breasts pressed against Melody as she enveloped her in a cloying embrace. Rhapsody's heated touch warmed Melody's shivering torso. "It's clear you were sent to me as a gift from the gods. You're our way out of that Underworld dungeon." Slowly, she rocked them from side to side.

"Can you imagine our race able to live unrestricted among the humans, feeding and breeding, remaining young and beautiful? So many of you are too young to remember how much power we used to possess. And how free we were. Don't you want that for your sisters? I do. Desperately. And it will start right here in San Francisco—birthplace of the new Siren."

Melody's breath caught in her throat. Rhapsody and the Sirens like her could never be allowed to escape and infect this realm.

"Now, Melody, *my savior.*" She wiped away the crusted blood on Melody's wounded cheek. "Let us find you a new human. You'll have to get rid of your plaything. He is an unacceptable risk." Rhapsody squeezed her gently. "But I'll help you with that. I can even end him for you, if you'd like. From this night on, you and I will do everything together. I'll make sure that soon, very soon, you begin to produce children so that my race, *our* race, is able to take its rightful place in this delicious world!" Her smile was feral. "But first, we'll go to the water. Show me how to merge a human life with mine."

Melody went very still inside. She focused, forcing her ivory skin to tingle and trade places with deep green scales. "Never!"

Without her golden shield and borrowed strength, Rhapsody was no different from the humans she despised. Into her hands, Melody channeled the pain from a lifetime of lies and her fears for the future. She thrust her palms against Rhapsody's sternum. Her naked body flew backward, crashing into the ground and rolling end over end.

Melody didn't wait to see if her rag doll body stirred. She tore through the plastic door, releasing her scales as she sprinted down the street. She let her feet carry her toward the one human she'd risk her life to protect—Dean.

CHAPTER FIFTEEN

Dean popped open the top of his third bottle of HUB IPA and hurried to the freezer to grab another cold beer stein, singing badly but enthusiastically along with the opening credits of *Criminal Minds*. "Gotta love a Netflix marathon," he told the beer as he tilted the glass and poured the amber liquid.

His doorbell buzzed insistently. Dean checked his watch—almost eleven thirty. Maybe it was Mel—"Dean! Let me in! Dean!"

He was off out of the kitchen and at the door in an instant. He wrenched it open and Melody hurled herself into his arms. Her hair and her body were soaked and she was dripping seawater all over him.

"We have to go. We have to leave. Now!" she heaved though uncontrollable sobs.

Visually, he cleared the hall before closing the door and locking it behind them. "What happened? Are you hurt?"

She shook her head, wet hair matted to her face. "We

have to leave," she repeated. "We can run away together. Just the two of us. Wouldn't you like that?"

He tried to make her sit, but she remained rigid. "Tell me what's going on. I can protect you, but I need details."

"I don't need protection. But you, you do."

"From what? What are you talking about?"

She brushed back her hair, revealing a red slash dissecting the pale flesh of her cheek.

"Jesus! You're bleeding. I'm getting my first aid kit." He turned for the bathroom, but she grabbed his wrist in a vise grip.

"She'll come for you, and when she finds you, she'll kill you."

Her solemnity made Dean's stomach clench. "Who?"

"Rhapsody."

"Your cousin?" A chuckle blew past his lips. "God, you had me really worried there for a minute." He sat back on the couch and ran a slightly trembling hand through his hair.

"What are you doing? Get up. We have to go!"

"Look, I know you have crazy family drama, but I'm not going to run away every time one of your jealous cousins comes into town. Now sit down and let me look at your cheek. I think you might need stitches."

She crossed her arms over her chest defiantly. "This is serious."

"And so is that cut on your face."

"I'll let you look at it only if you promise we'll leave if she finds this place."

"Would it make you feel better if we went to the roof? We can see the whole street from up there."

"That sounds nice," she said, sounding a little more like herself.

"I'll grab a blanket and light the fire pit so you can dry off. Why are you all wet, anyway?"

"It was Rhapsody," she muttered.

Dean snagged the throw from the back of the couch and they went through the kitchen and out his back door, and climbed the flight of stairs that led to the rooftop patio area attached to his condo. "Did she do that to your cheek too?" He wrapped the blanket around her shoulders, guiding her to the wide, comfortable chaise he'd bought just a week before because Melody loved spending time up there, gazing out at the bay with him. He lit the fire pit and hurried back to her, pulling her close to him.

"Tell me," he said.

"This is really hard for me to talk about." She paused, lifting a shaky hand to brush back a damp curl. "I'm afraid it'll never be the same between us once I tell you."

He took her trembling hand and kissed it lightly. "Melody, there is nothing you could tell me about your family that would make me change how I feel about you."

"How do you feel about me?"

He hesitated, caught off guard by the directness of her question. She'd spent the past month avoiding the subject of feelings between them, and that had become their norm— spending almost every day together, and talking about everything *except* her family and their relationship.

"Never mind. I shouldn't have—"

"I love you!" he interrupted. "Although I hadn't planned on yelling it at you like that. I'd planned on telling you after

I filled you full of my Nana's famous spaghetti and, maybe, coaxed you to drink too much wine."

Normally, she would have laughed and teased him about the famous Nana spaghetti he'd already attempted to make for her—and managed to totally ruin with sticky, overcooked pasta. That night, Melody's full lips didn't so much as begin to lift in her familiar, beautiful smile. That night, Melody stared into his eyes as if she were trying to see through them to his soul.

"What does love mean to you?" she asked.

He blinked in surprise, but his response came easily. "Love means being willing to make her needs as important as yours, and accepting her completely—faults and all."

She nodded somberly. "That's what I think it means, too." Melody drew a deep breath and let it out with a long sigh, and as she did she lifted her chin and squared her shoulders. "I have to tell you two things, and then I need to show you something so that I'm sure you understand."

"First, could you tell me what happened to you tonight? You look like it was something pretty bad."

"It was—it is. And that's part of what I have to tell you—show you."

"Okay," Dean said hesitantly.

"I love you too. That's the first thing I need to say to you."

Pressure he hadn't realized had been squeezing his chest lifted, and his grin was so wide it almost hurt. "That's good to hear, Melody. *Really* good to hear. Does that mean you'll actually say yes to being my date at my sister's wedding this weekend?"

"Yes," she said firmly. "If you still want me after tonight."

Dean took both of her hands in his. "Melody, you are the only woman I want—tonight, tomorrow, next year, and next decade. That won't change. No matter what."

Melody's emerald eyes glistened. "Promise?"

He wiped a tear from her smooth cheek. "Promise."

"Oh, Dean! I do love you! I love you so much!" She wrapped her arms around him and pressed into him, raining kisses all over his face.

He laughed again, trying to capture her mouth—and then her lips found his and everything changed. After that first night, when he'd moved too fast and frightened her, Dean had been taking it slow—really slow. He made sure he followed her lead. Sometimes they'd curl up on his couch, or here, by the fire pit, and he'd hold her while she kissed him. Lately, she'd been doing a lot of exploring—three nights ago she'd actually asked him, shyly and sweetly, to take off his shirt. He'd happily complied, and then had thoroughly enjoyed her hesitant caresses, being careful not to do anything that might spoil the sense of trust and safety he'd built between them.

That night her kisses changed, and so did her caresses. Neither were hesitant. Her eager mouth consumed him, asking for more as her tongue teased in time with hands that reached under his shirt, gliding up to find his sensitive nipples and then down to the waist of his jeans, where her clever fingers played over his trembling skin.

Slowly, he found the edge of her top, letting his fingers move up and under to the unbelievably warm, unbearably soft skin beneath it.

Melody moaned against his mouth. "Yes, Dean, touch me. I want you to."

Finally, Dean allowed his hands to follow his fantasies. They dipped under her shirt, softly caressing the smooth, curved line of her waist up and up until he found the fullness of her breasts. She arched into his touch, gasping in pleasure as he teased her taut nipples.

"Dean! I—I have to show you something. Have to tell you something."

"Anything, Melody—you can show me, tell me, anything."

Dean kissed a line up her neck, loving the seductive scent of salt and sea that always clung to her skin. He was so mesmerized by the taste and touch of her that he almost didn't notice when she began to change.

Almost.

Beneath his eager lips her skin twitched. The thought that surfaced from his passion-fogged mind was that it reminded him of what a horse's skin did when it flicked off flies, and that one, strange thought was enough to cause him to pause—to lean back—to look at Melody.

At first he couldn't comprehend what he was seeing, and he just stared. Something was happening to her— something terrible.

Melody's skin wasn't actually twitching. It was changing. What had been soft, seductive flesh was now covered with green scales—smooth and supple like a snake. His shocked gaze went to her face. Her hair! Her beautiful, strawberry blonde hair had disappeared, and in its place was an undulating mass of copper tentacles.

Dean's head swiveled back and forth, back and forth. The fear hit him then—hard and deep in his gut. He tried to fight against it—tried to think through the panic and make sense out of what was happening, but the horror was visceral, uncontrollable, and overwhelming.

He surged from the chaise, stumbling against the fire pit and almost knocking it over.

"Dean! Be careful!"

The voice was still hers, but it echoed from a mouth that was now ringed with sharp, glistening teeth.

"No! No, no, no!" He heard himself speaking, but it seemed as if the sounds were coming from another person.

"Dean, it's okay—I promise. It's just me. This is the *real* me. It's what I've been trying to tell you—show you."

"No! This can't be real! It can't be happening. You're— you're..." He forced his gaze from her teeth to her eyes. They were huge emerald orbs in which he saw nothing but his terrified reflection. "Oh, God! You're not even human!"

Water spilled from her strange eyes, washing down her jewel-colored cheeks. She stood and took a hesitant step forward. Terror spiked from deep within him. Dean staggered back so quickly that he tripped and almost fell.

"I'm sorry! So, so sorry!" Melody spoke imploringly. "Please don't be afraid of me. I can explain this—I can explain all of this, just sit down and give me a chance."

"What are you?" Dean heard himself ask, though he wasn't sure how he was still able to speak, as an overwhelming and instinctual need to get away from her consumed him.

"I'm a Siren," she said.

"You're a monster!" he shouted.

"Dean, it's *me*. I'm still the Melody you love and who loves you right back. None of that has changed."

"*Everything* has changed!"

"No!" she sobbed brokenly. "You said love means accepting me completely! Please, please just sit with me."

As she spoke, the creature that had been Melody reached toward him, as if to embrace him with her arms of scales and her green hands—hands that Dean saw were no longer human, but tipped with pointed claws, as sharp and deadly looking as her fangs, which glistened dangerously at him as she smiled a cruel parody of the beautiful expression he had come to crave—come to love.

"Come on," she coaxed, her sweet, familiar voice suddenly grotesque as it came from the hideous maw. "It's okay, Dean. Come here to me. I would never, ever hurt you." Still baring her teeth in that terrible smile, she moved to him, reaching to take his hand.

"No! Stay back!" he shouted.

Adrenaline surged through his body as his survival instinct kicked into overdrive. Dean lurched back suddenly, violently, to avoid her grasping touch, and the lip of the rooftop balcony caught him hard in the back of his thighs, knocking him off balance. Frantically, his arms windmilled into empty air as he tried to regain his balance, but there was nothing—nothing at all except a horrible plummeting sensation joined eternally with an otherworldly, inhuman sound that filled his senses, blanketing him from reality.

Dean fell.

He didn't feel the pain of landing on the concrete sidewalk two stories below. He didn't feel anything. All of his senses were focused on the creature that used to be Melody as she stared down at him, sobbing and keening into the night.

She does love me, Dean thought. He blinked tears from his eyes, and tried to sit up, but found he had no control over his body. *And I love her—unconditionally.* He stared up at his Siren, and really saw her.

She was different, and yet she was still Melody. He could see that now, and his fading mind wondered why she had seemed so terrifying to him. Why hadn't he sat beside her and let her explain? *She wouldn't have hurt me. She would never have hurt me.* As the world began to darken around him, Dean understood. Her change had made him react on an automatic, instinctive level, and he hadn't been able to reason through the fight-or-flight impulse. But encroaching death brought one gift—the ability to see through his reflexive response and find his Melody within the strangeness of the Siren.

With a last, superhuman effort, Dean lifted his arm, reaching his hand up toward her.

Melody's reaction was instantaneous. She leaped to stand on the lip of the balcony, and then she jumped.

"No!" He tried to shout, but the word came out as a whisper.

But she didn't fall to the pavement and land broken and dying beside him. She landed lightly, gracefully, in a crouch several yards from him.

"I won't come near you," she sobbed. "I'll get help!"

She started to turn away, but he managed to lift his hand again, reaching toward her. "Don't go," he whispered through the blood that frothed from his mouth.

She came to him then, falling to her knees beside him. "I—I can't change back—not while I can't control my emotions." She bowed her head and tears pooled with his blood. "Forgive me. Please forgive me."

Dean fought against the rising tide of darkness narrowing his vision. *I can't leave her like this.*

"Melody," he whispered. "Look at me."

She lifted her head.

He turned his hand to her, and she took it gently between hers. Her sea-green skin was warm and soft, and her claws rested carefully, harmlessly, against his fingers.

"I love you," he said.

A sob tore from her throat, and she shook her head, the copper tendrils swaying around her. "No, you can't. This is what happens when a human loves a Siren. I thought I was different—I thought we could be different. I was so, so wrong."

Dean tried to smile, but he couldn't feel his mouth—all he could feel was a deep, dangerous cold creeping through his broken body. "I do love you. We *are* different."

"You're dying because of me," she cried.

"And yet I will love you forever." His body spasmed then, and he coughed as blood filled his mouth. His vision dimmed even more as the world around him began to fade. "I—I thought you were a sea goddess the first time I saw you. I was right."

She bent to him, resting her head on his chest as she held him and sobbed. "I love you, Dean. Always."

"Then find me again, my sea goddess."

She lifted her head so that he could look into her eyes. They blazed with an inhuman emerald light that suddenly filled Dean with the sweet solace of hope. "I swear to you on the blood of my immortal ancestors that I will find you, Dean Kent, and when I do we will never be parted again."

"I will hold you to your oath for an eternity..."

Then his fading sight went black, his breath fled his body, and Dean Kent died in the arms of his Siren.

EPILOGUE

"W-why are you doing this? I'll give you what you want. *Anything!*" The woman had finally stopped kicking and squirming and pummeling Rhapsody's back with bony fingers. "Please," she sobbed. "Please, let me go. I won't tell anyone. I won't! I just want to go home. Please!"

Rhapsody's insides warmed with each cry from the sniveling woman she carried over her shoulder toward the water's edge. It had been too long since she'd made a human beg for its life.

The water was waist deep and inky black. Rhapsody slid the woman down the front of her glistening, gold body until she cradled her like a child. Swollen, frightened eyes stared up at her, and Rhapsody smiled.

"I'm sending you home." She dropped her into the frigid ocean water, catching her by the cheap, sequined jean jacket that'd drawn her attention under the dim streetlight of Fort Mason Park. Women were almost as easy to subdue as men. They were weak, so weak—the entire species.

Water splashed her face as the woman resumed flailing. Rhapsody cringed and felt the skin around her eyes and brow wrinkle like the flesh of a decaying peach. She'd been at this for more than a year. Back and forth to the Mortal Realm. Each time lengthening her stay. Each time growing older and less beautiful. She needed to retreat to Tartarus and restore her rapidly aging visage, but she couldn't. Not yet. Not until she'd completed her quest.

She forced the writhing, burbling body deeper under the waves, her grip tightening around the jacket's collar as the woman struggled to free herself. She clawed at Rhapsody's scaly arms and salt burned the gashes and scratches, but it didn't faze her. The Siren was consumed by the need to recreate what had come so easily to that insipid Melody.

"She didn't deserve your gift, you fools!" Rhapsody cursed whichever gods took the time to listen. Her lips curled and puckered like fractures in parched earth. "But I will get mine. I'll take human life and become more than she is!"

After that night in the warehouse, when Rhapsody had discovered how to undo the curse oppressing her race, Melody had disappeared into the stinking abyss that was the overpopulated city. Not that that mattered. Rhapsody knew what she had to do—she didn't need that weak child to guide her. "I'll be greater and more powerful than she ever will."

Garbled screams bubbled up from black water. Rhapsody cackled as the woman's nails sank into her wrists. "Keep trying! It's more enjoyable when you struggle!" she roared, and plunged her deeper under the dark water.

The thrashing stilled. The muted chokes quieted. Gentle pulsing waves rocked Rhapsody and the woman. She released the body. The woman's lifeless limbs rose to the surface, peeking through the ebony water like cream in coffee.

Rhapsody patted the skin around her aging eyes. "Huh, nothing." She smoothed down her hair and wiped at the mascara streaking her face. "Well, you know what they say in this realm—if at first you don't succeed, try, try again."

ACKNOWLEDGEMENTS

We would like to thank our wonderful agent and friend, Meredith Bernstein. She's the reason Team Cast exists!

Thank you to our publisher, Diversion Books, for being so enthusiastic about this novella. We appreciate you! Go Team Cast!

A big thanks to the Fairmont Residences at Ghirardelli Square in San Francisco for making our research stays divine.

From P.C.: I want to thank my daughter, Kristin, for being so brilliant and simply fabulous in all ways. Shall we have celebratory luncheon now?

From Kristin: I want to thank my mam, P.C., for being absolutely amazing and not too obnoxious when I cut some of her beautiful words. Let's luncheon!

And to you—yes, YOU! Your choices are powerful. Thank you for choosing us. And remember, be kind to yourself.

PHOTO CREDIT: STARK PHOTOGRAPHY

KRISTIN CAST is a #1 *New York Times* and #1 *USA Today* bestselling author who teamed with her mother to write the wildly successful House of Night series. She has editorial credits, a thriving T-shirt line, and a passion for all things paranormal. When away from her writing desk, Kristin loves going on adventures with her friends, family, and significant other, playing with her French bulldogs, and discovering new hobbies. This year she'll work on gardening, cooking, and renovating her house.

P.C. CAST is a #1 *New York Times* and #1 *USA Today* bestselling author and a member of the Oklahoma Writers Hall of Fame. Her novels have been awarded the prestigious: Oklahoma Book Award, YALSA Quick Pick for Reluctant Readers, *Romantic Times* Reviewers' Choice Award, the Prism, Holt Medallion, Daphne du Maurier, Booksellers' Best, and the Laurel Wreath. P.C. is an experienced teacher and talented speaker. Ms. Cast lives in Oregon near her fabulous daughter, with her adorable pack of dogs, her crazy Maine Coon, and a bunch of horses.

CPSIA information can be obtained
at www.ICGtesting.com
Printed in the USA
BVOW04s1002301016

466164BV00002B/3/P

9 781682 303436